D1465789

THE GHOSTLY TALES
OF
WASHINGTON IRVING

Other books edited by Michael Hayes

THE SUPERNATURAL SHORT STORIES OF
ROBERT LOUIS STEVENSON

THE SUPERNATURAL SHORT STORIES OF
SIR WALTER SCOTT

THE SUPERNATURAL SHORT STORIES OF
CHARLES DICKENS

THE FANTASTIC TALES OF FITZ-JAMES O'BRIEN

SUPERNATURAL POETRY:
A Selection: 16th Cent to the 20th Cent.

THE GHOSTLY TALES
OF
WASHINGTON IRVING

Edited with an introduction by
Michael Hayes

JOHN CALDER · LONDON
RIVERRUN PRESS · DALLAS

First published in Great Britain 1979 by
John Calder (Publishers) Ltd.,
18 Brewer Street, London W1R 4AS
First published in the U.S.A. 1979 by
Riverrun Press Inc.
4951 Top Line Drive, Dallas, Texas 75247

ISBN 0 7145 3739 X casebound

Library of Congress cataloguing card
No. 79-64438

Typeset in 11 on 12 point Baskerville by Woolaston Parker Ltd., Leicester.
Printed by M & A Thomson Litho Ltd., East Kilbride, Scotland.
Bound by Hunter & Foulis Ltd., Edinburgh.

CONTENTS

To
Colm Hayes
by way of thanks

INTRODUCTION

*Indeed he was the American of his time universally known. This
modest and kindly man was the creator of Diedrich Knickerbocker
and Rip Van Winkle. He was the father of our literature and at
that time its patriarch. He was Washington Irving.*

George William Curtis.

Washington Irving was born on April 3, 1783 in New York, the
son of a Scottish father and an English mother who had earlier
emigrated to the New World, and where industrious father
William had become a prosperous merchant. A delicate child
blessed with a healthy temperament, the youngest of eleven
children, he grew up in this closely knit middle-class family,
against a background rich in religious and literary influences.

Although his formal education was rather sketchy, or perhaps
because of it, he was receptive to new knowledge and fresh
influences offered him, as he watched the hustle and bustle of the
city of New York growing around him.

His first literary effort at the age of twenty was a series of light
and lively essays which appeared under the collective title, *The
Letters of Jonathan Oldstyle Esq.*

Concerned with his failing health, his family sent him to
Europe in 1804. He returned two years later with bulging
notebooks, brimming with health, and determined to be a
writer. His *Diedrich Knickerbocker's History of New York* published
in 1809 is still hailed as the first great comic book in American

literature. Over the years, both at home and during lengthy periods spent in Europe, Irving produced other works including his *Tales of a Traveller, Life and Voyages of Columbus, The Conquest of Granada, The Alhambra, Oliver Goldsmith, Mahomet and his Successors,* and finally his *Life of George Washington,* upon which he laboured until shortly before his death on November 28, 1859. But it was *The Sketchbook of Geoffrey Crayon Gent,* published in 1820, which firmly established Irving's literary reputation. Widely praised on both sides of the Atlantic, this volume contained two of his most famous and enduring tales, *Rip Van Winkle* and *The Legend of Sleepy Hollow.*

Even at the height of his success, however, when he was acclaimed by Scott, Byron, Moore, Dickens and Coleridge, Washington Irving found many detractors to accuse him of plagiarism, and to point out that most of his works were adaptations or versions of existing books or folk tales. Being a gentle and modest man acutely aware of his shortcomings, Irving never sought to deny this. Indeed his skilful pen often searched desperately for something to write about; but if there is so little room left for pure imagination in his writings, it is assuredly because he found the spectacle of real life around him entirely absorbing. He loved people and never tired of watching them, with an affectionate and slightly mischievous eye. His work is rich in keenly observed detail; and since the writer is a warm, kindly man, the humour is gentle, the satire never cruel.

Prompted by the often encountered view that Irving 'is not much read nowadays', I have sought to introduce him to a wider audience by putting together a collection of his best tales. Barring *Rip Van Winkle* and *The Legend of Sleepy Hollow* which are well known, and have been constantly in print since their first publication, this selection presents ten stories which, I believe, deserve to be revived and appreciated anew.

As for Washington Irving's rightful place in the world of literature, the final word belongs to William Makepeace Thackeray who hailed him as 'the first ambassador whom the New World of Letters sent to the Old.'

Michael Hayes

THE KNIGHT OF MALTA

In the course of a tour in Sicily, in the days of my juvenility, I
passed some little time at the ancient city of Catania, at the foot
of Mount Etna. Here I became acquainted with the Chevalier
L———, an old knight of Malta. It was not many years after the
time that Napoleon had dislodged the knights from their island,
and he still wore the insignia of his order. He was not, however,
one of those reliques of that once chivalrous body, who have
been described as 'a few worn-out old men, creeping about
certain parts of Europe, with the Maltese cross on their breasts;'
on the contrary, though advanced in life, his form was still light
and vigorous: he had a pale, thin, intellectual visage, with a high
forehead, and a bright, visionary eye. He seemed to take a fancy
to me, as I certainly did to him, and we soon became intimate. I
visited him occasionally, at his apartments, in the wing of an old
palace, looking toward Mount Etna. He was an antiquary, a
virtuoso, and a connoisseur. His rooms were decorated with
mutilated statues, dug up from Grecian and Roman ruins; old
vases, lachrymals, and sepulchral lamps. He had astronomical
and chemical instruments, and black-letter books in various
languages. I found that he had dipped a little in chimerical
studies, and had a hankering after astrology and alchemy. He
affected to believe in dreams and visions, and delighted in the
fanciful Rosicrucian doctrines. I cannot persuade myself,
however, that he really believed in all these; I rather think he

loved to let his imagination carry him away into the boundless fairy land which they unfolded.

In company with the chevalier, I made several excursions on horseback about the environs of Catania and the picturesque skirts of Mount Etna. One of these led through a village, which had sprung up on the very track of an ancient eruption, the houses being built of lava. At one time we passed, for some distance, along a narrow lane, between two high dead convent walls. It was a cut-throat looking place, in a country where assassinations are frequent; and just about midway through it, we observed blood upon the pavement and the walls, as if a murder had actually been committed there.

The chevalier spurred on his horse, until he had extricated himself completely from this suspicious neighbourhood. He then observed, that it reminded him of a similar blind alley in Malta, infamous on account of the many assassinations that had taken place there; concerning one of which he related a long and tragical story, that lasted until we reached Catania. It involved various circumstances of a wild and supernatural character, but which he assured me were handed down in tradition, and generally credited by the old inhabitants of Malta.

As I like to pick up strange stories, and as I was particularly struck with several parts of this, I made a minute of it, on my return to my lodgings. The memorandum was lost, with several of my travelling papers, and the story had faded from my mind, when recently, on perusing a French memoir, I came suddenly upon it, dressed up, it is true, in a very different manner, but agreeing in the leading facts, and given upon the word of that famous adventurer the Count Cagliostro.

I have amused myself, during a snowy day in the country, by rendering it roughly into English, for the entertainment of a youthful circle round the Christmas fire. It was well received by my auditors, who, however, are rather easily pleased. One proof of its merits is, that it sent some of the youngest of them quaking to their beds, and gave them very fearful dreams. Hoping that it may have the same effect upon the ghost-hunting reader, I subjoin it. I would observe, that wherever I have modified the

French version of the story, it has been in conformity to some recollection of the narrative of my friend, the Knight of Malta.

☙❦☙

THE GRAND PRIOR OF MINORCA
A veritable ghost story

> *Keep my wits, heaven! They say spirits appear*
> *To melancholy minds, and the graves open!*
> Fletcher

About the middle of last century, while the Knights of Saint John of Jerusalem still maintained something of their ancient state and sway in the island of Malta, a tragical event took place there, which is the groundwork of the following narrative.

It may be as well to premise, that at the time we are treating of, the Order of Saint John of Jerusalem, grown excessively wealthy, had degenerated from its originally devout and warlike character. Instead of being a hardy body of 'monk-knights,' sworn soldiers of the Cross, fighting the Paynim in the Holy Land, or scouring the Mediterranean and scourging the Barbary coasts with their galleys, or feeding the poor and attending upon the sick at their hospitals, they led a life of luxury and libertinism, and were to be found in the most voluptuous Courts of Europe. The order, in fact, had become a mode of providing for the needy branches of the Catholic aristocracy of Europe. 'A commandery,' we are told, was a splendid provision for a younger brother; and men of rank, however dissolute, provided they belonged to the highest aristocracy, became Knights of Malta, just as they did bishops, or colonels of regiments, or Court chamberlains. After a brief residence at Malta, the knights passed the rest of their time in their own countries, or only made a visit now and then to the island. While there, having but little military duty to perform, they beguiled their idleness by paying attentions to the fair.

There was one circle of society, however, into which they could not obtain currency. This was composed of a few families of the old Maltese nobility, natives of the island. These families, not being permitted to enrol any of their members in the order, affected to hold no intercourse with its chevaliers; admitting none into their exclusive coteries but the Grand Master, whom they acknowledged as their sovereign, and the members of the chapter which composed his council.

To indemnify themselves for this exclusion, the chevaliers carried their gallantries into the next class of society, composed of those who held civil, administrative, and judicial situations. The ladies of this class were called *honorate*, or honourables, to distinguish them from the inferior orders; and among them were many of superior grace, beauty, and fascination.

Even in this hospitable class, the chevaliers were not all equally favoured. Those of Germany had the decided preference, owing to their fair and fresh complexions, and the kindliness of their manners: next to these came the Spanish cavaliers, on account of their profound and courteous devotion, and most discreet secrecy. Singular as it may seem, the chevaliers of France fared the worst. The Maltese ladies dreaded their volatility, and their proneness to boast of their amours, and shunned all entanglement with them. They were forced, therefore, to content themselves with conquests among females of the lower orders. They revenged themselves, after the gay French manner, by making the *honorate* the objects of all kinds of jests and mystifications; by prying into their tender affairs with the more favoured chevaliers, and making them the theme of song and epigram.

About this time, a French vessel arrived at Malta, bringing out a distinguished personage of the Order of Saint John of Jerusalem, the Commander de Foulquerre, who came to solicit the post of commander-in-chief of the galleys. He was descended from an old and warrior line of French nobility, his ancestors having long been seneschals of Poiton, and claiming descent from the Counts of Angouleme.

The arrival of the commander caused a little uneasiness among the peaceably inclined, for he bore the character, in the island, of being fiery, arrogant, and quarrelsome. He had already been three times at Malta, and on each visit had signalized himself by some rash and deadly affray. As he was now thirty-five years of age, however, it was hoped that time might have taken off the fiery edge of his spirit, and that he might prove more quiet and sedate than formerly. The commander set up an establishment befitting his rank and pretentions; for he arrogated to himself an importance greater even than that of the Grand Master. His house immediately became the rallying point of all the young French chevaliers. They informed him of all the slights they had experienced or imagined, and indulged their petulant and satirical vein at the expense of the *honorate* and their admirers. The chevaliers of other nations soon found the topics and tone of conversation at the commander's irksome and offensive, and gradually ceased to visit there. The commander remained at the head of a national *clique*, who looked up to him as their model. If he was not as boisterous and quarrelsome as formerly, he had become haughty and overbearing. He was fond of talking over his past affairs of punctilio and bloody duel. When walking the streets, he was generally attended by a ruffling train of young French chevaliers, who caught his own air of assumption and bravado. These he would conduct to the scenes of his deadly encounters, point out the very spot where each fatal lunge had been given, and dwell vaingloriously on every particular.

Under his tuition the young French chevaliers began to add bluster and arrogance to their former petulance and levity; they fired up on the most trivial occasions, particularly with those who had been most successful with the fair, and would put on the most intolerable drawcansir airs. The other chevaliers conducted themselves with all possible forbearance and reserve; but they saw it would be impossible to keep on long in this manner, without coming to an open rupture.

Among the Spanish cavaliers was one named Don Luis de Lima Vasconcellos. He was distantly related to the Grand Master, and had been enrolled at an early age among his pages, but had been rapidly promoted by him, until, at the age of twenty-six, he had been given the richest Spanish commandery in the order. He had, moreover, been fortunate with the fair, with one of whom, the most beautiful *honorata* of Malta, he had long maintained the most tender correspondence.

The character, rank, and connections of Don Luis put him on a par with the imperious Commander de Foulquerre, and pointed him out as a leader and champion to his countrymen. The Spanish cavaliers repaired to him, therefore, in a body; represented all the grievances they had sustained, and the evils they apprehended, and urged him to use his influence with the commander and his adherents to put a stop to the growing abuses.

Don Luis was gratified by this mark of confidence and esteem on the part of his countrymen, and promised to have an interview with the Commander de Foulquerre on the subject. He resolved to conduct himself with the utmost caution and delicacy on the occasion; to represent to the commander the evil consequences which might result from the inconsiderate conduct of the young French chevaliers, and to entreat him to exert the great influence he so deservedly possessed over them, to restrain their excesses. Don Luis was aware, however, of the peril that attended any interview of the kind with this imperious and fractious man, and apprehended, however it might commence, that it would terminate in a dual. Still it was an affair of honour, in which Castilian dignity was concerned; beside, he had a lurking disgust at the overbearing manners of de Foulquerre, and perhaps had been somewhat offended by certain intrusive attentions which he had presumed to pay to the beautiful *honorata*.

It was now Holy Week; a time too sacred for worldly feuds and passions, especially in a community under the dominion of a religious order: it was agreed, therefore, that the dangerous interview in question should not take place until after the Easter holy days. It is probable, from subsequent circumstances, that the Commander de Foulquerre had some information of this arrangement among the Spanish cavaliers, and was determined to be beforehand, and to mortify the pride of their champion, who was thus preparing to read him a lecture. He chose Good

Friday for his purpose. On this sacred day it is customary, in Catholic countries, to make a tour of all the churches, offering up prayers in each. In every Catholic church, as is well known, there is a vessel of holy water near the door. In this every one, on entering, dips his fingers, and makes therewith the sign of the cross on his forehead and breast. An office of gallantry, among the young Spaniards, is to stand near the door, dip their hands in the holy vessel, and extend them courteously and respectfully to any lady of their acquaintance who may enter: who thus receives the sacred water at second hand, on the tips of their fingers, and proceeds to cross herself with all due decorum. The Spaniards, who are the most jealous of lovers, are impatient when this piece of devotional gallantry is proffered to the object of their affections by any other hand: on Good Friday, therefore, when a lady makes a tour of the churches, it is the usage among them for the inamorato to follow her from church to church, so as to present her the holy water at the door of each; thus testifying his own devotion, and at the same time preventing the officious services of a rival.

On the day in question Don Luis followed the beautiful *honorata*, to whom, as has already been observed, he had long been devoted. At the very first church she visited, the Commander de Foulquerre was stationed at the portal, with several of the young French chevaliers about him. Before Don Luis could offer her the holy water he was anticipated by the commander, who thrust himself between them, and, while he performed the gallant office to the lady, rudely turned his back upon her admirer, and trod upon his feet. This insult was enjoyed by the young Frenchmen who were present: it was too deep and grave to be forgiven by Spanish pride; and at once put an end to all Don Luis's plans of caution and forbearance. He repressed his passion for the moment, however, and waited until all the parties left the church; then, accosting the commander with an air of coolness and unconcern, he inquired after his health, and asked to what church he proposed making his second visit. 'To the Magisterial Church of St. John.' Don Luis offered to conduct him thither, by the shortest route. His offer

was accepted, apparently without suspicion, and they proceeded together. After walking some distance, they entered a
long, narrow lane, without door or window opening upon it,
called the 'Strada Stretta', or narrow street. It was a street in
which duels were tacitly permitted, or connived at, in Malta,
and were suffered to pass as accidental encounters. Everywhere
else they were prohibited. This restriction had been instituted to
diminish the number of duels formerly so frequent in Malta. As
a farther precaution, to render these encounters less fatal, it was
an offence, punishable with death, for any one to enter this street
armed with either poniard or pistol. It was a lonely, dismal
street, just wide enough for two men to stand upon their guard
and cross their swords; few persons ever traversed it, unless with
some sinister design; and on any preconcerted duello the seconds
posted themselves at each end, to stop all passengers and prevent
interruptions.

In the present instance, the parties had scarce entered the
street, when Don Luis drew his sword, and called upon the
commander to defend himself.

De Foulquerre was evidently taken by surprise: he drew back,
and attempted to expostulate; but Don Luis persisted in defying
him to the combat.

After a second or two, he likewise drew his sword, but
immediately lowered the point.

'Good Friday!' ejaculated he, shaking his head: 'one word
with you; it is full six years since I have been in a confessional: I
am shocked at the state of my conscience; but within three
days—that is to say, on Monday next—'

Don Luis would listen to nothing. Though naturally of a
peaceable disposition, he had been stung to fury, and people of
that character when once incensed, are deaf to reason. He
compelled the commander to put himself on his guard. The
latter, though a man accustomed to brawl and battle, was
singularly dismayed. Terror was visible in all his features. He
placed himself with his back to the wall, and the weapons were
crossed. The contest was brief and fatal. At the very first thrust,
the sword of Don Luis passed through the body of his antagonist.

The commander staggered to the wall, and leaned against it. 'On Good Friday!' ejaculated he again, with a failing voice, and despairing accents. 'Heaven pardon you!' added he; 'take my sword to Têtefoulques, and have a hundred masses performed in the chapel of the castle, for the repose of my soul!' With these words he expired.

The fury of Don Luis was at an end. He stood aghast, gazing at the bleeding body of the commander. He called to mind the prayer of the deceased for three days' respite, to make his peace with heaven; he had refused it; had sent him to the grave, with all his sins upon his head! His conscience smote him to the core; he gathered up the sword of the commander, which he had been enjoined to take to Têtefoulques, and hurried from the fatal Strada Stretta.

The duel of course made a great noise in Malta, but had no injurious effect on the worldly fortunes of Don Luis. He made a full declaration of the whole matter before the proper authorities; the chapter of the order considered it one of those casual encounters of the Strada Stretta, which were mourned over, but tolerated; the public, by whom the late commander had been generally detested, declared that he deserved his fate. It was but three days after the event, that Don Luis was advanced to one of the highest dignities of the order, being invested by the Grand Master with the Priorship of the kingdom of Minorca.

From that time forward, however, the whole character and conduct of Don Luis underwent a change. He became a prey to a dark melancholy, which nothing could assuage. The most austere piety, the severest penances, had no effect in allaying the horror which preyed upon his mind. He was absent for a long time from Malta; having gone, it was said, on remote pilgrimages: when he returned, he was more haggard than ever. There seemed something mysterious and inexplicable in this disorder of mind. The following is the revelation made by himself, of the horrible visions or chimeras by which he was haunted.

'When I had made my declaration before the chapter,' said

he, 'my provocations were publicly known; I had made my peace with man; but it was not so with God, nor with my confessor, nor with my own conscience. My act was doubly criminal, from the day on which it was committed, and from my refusal to a delay of three days, for the victim of my resentment to receive the sacraments. His despairing ejaculation, "Good Friday! Good Friday!" continually rang in my ears, "Why did I not grant the respite!" cried I to myself; "was it not enough to kill the body, but must I seek to kill the soul!"

'On the night following Friday I started suddenly from my sleep. An unaccountable horror was upon me. I looked wildly around. It seemed as if I were not in my apartment, nor in my bed, but in the fatal Strada Stretta, lying on the pavement. I again saw the commander leaning against the wall; I again heard his dying words: "Take my sword to Têtefoulques, and have a hundred masses performed in the chapel of the castle, for the repose of my soul!"

'On the following night I caused one of my servants to sleep in the same room with me. I saw and heard nothing, either on that night or any of the following, until the next Friday, when I had again the same vision, with this difference, that my valet seemed to be lying some distance from me on the pavement of the Strada Stretta. The vision continued to be repeated on every Friday night, the commander always appearing in the same manner, and uttering the same words: "Take my sword to Têtefoulques, and have a hundred masses performed in the chapel of the castle, for the repose of my soul!"

'On questioning my servant on the subject, he stated, that on these occasions he dreamed that he was lying in a very narrow street, but he neither saw nor heard anything of the commander.

'I knew nothing of this Têtefoulques, whither the defunct was so urgent I should carry his sword. I made inquiries, therefore, concerning it, among the French chevaliers. They informed me that it was an old castle, situated about four leagues from Poitiers, in the midst of a forest. It had been built in old times, several centuries since, by Foulques Taillefer, (or Fulke Hack-iron,) a redoubtable hard-fighting Count of

Angouleme, who gave it to an illegitimate son, afterwards created Grand Seneschal of Poitou, which son became the progenitor of the Foulquerres of Têtefoulques, hereditary seneschals of Poitou. They farther informed me, that strange stories were told of this old castle, in the surrounding country, and that it contained many curious reliques. Among these were the arms of Foulques Taillefer, together with those of the warriors he had slain; and that it was an immemorial usage with the Foulquerres to have the weapons deposited there, which they had wielded either in war or single combat. This, then, was the reason of the dying injunction of the commander respecting his sword. I carried this weapon with me wherever I went, but still I neglected to comply with his request.

'The vision still continued to harass me with undiminished horror. I repaired to Rome, where I confessed myself to the Grand Cardinal Penitentiary, and informed him of the terrors with which I was haunted. He promised me absolution, after I should have performed certain acts of penance, the principal of which was to execute the dying request of the commander, by carrying his sword to Têtefoulques, and having the hundred masses performed in the chapel of the castle for the repose of his soul.

'I set out for France as speedily as possible, and made no delay in my journey. On arriving at Poitiers, I found that the tidings of the death of the commander had reached there, but had caused no more affliction than among the people of Malta. Leaving my equipage in the town, I put on the garb of a pilgrim, and taking a guide, set out on foot for Têtefoulques. Indeed the roads in this part of the country were impracticable for carriages.

'I found the castle of Têtefoulques a grand but gloomy and dilapidated pile. All the gates were closed, and there reigned over the whole place an air of almost savage loneliness and desertion. I had understood that its only inhabitants were the concierge or warder, and a kind of hermit who had charge of the chapel. After ringing for some time at the gate, I at length succeeded in bringing forth the warder, who bowed with reverence to my pilgrim's garb. I begged him to conduct me to the chapel, that being the end of my pilgrimage. We found the hermit there, chanting the funeral service; a dismal sound to one who came to perform a penance for the death of a member of the family. When he had ceased to chant, I informed him that I came to accomplish an obligation of conscience, and that I wished him to perform a hundred masses for the repose of the soul of the commander. He replied that, not being in orders, he was not authorised to perform mass, but that he would willingly undertake to see that my debt of conscience was discharged. I laid my offering on the altar, and would have placed the sword of the commander there, likewise. "Hold!" said the hermit, with a melancholy shake of the head, "this is no place for so deadly a weapon, that has so often been bathed in Christian blood. Take it to the armoury; you will find there trophies enough of like character. It is a place into which I never enter."

'The warder here took up the theme abandoned by the peaceful man of God. He assured me that I would see in the armoury the swords of all the warrior race of Foulquerres, together with those of the enemies over whom they had triumphed. This, he observed, had been a usage kept up since the time of Mellusine, and of her husband, Geoffrey à la Granddent, or Geoffrey with the Great tooth.

'I followed the gossiping warder to the armoury. It was a great dusty hall, hung round with Gothic-looking portraits of a stark line of warriors, each with his weapon, and the weapons of those he had slain in battle, hung beside his picture. The most conspicuous portrait was that of Foulques Taillefer, (Fulke Hack-iron,) Count of Angouleme, and founder of the castle. He was represented at full length, armed cap-à-pie, and grasping a huge buckler, on which were emblazoned three lions passant. The figure was so striking, that it seemed ready to start from the canvas: and I observed beneath this picture, a trophy composed of many weapons, proofs of the numberous triumphs of this hard-fighting old cavalier. Besides the weapons connected with the portraits, there were swords of all shapes, sizes, and centuries, hung round the hall; with piles of armour, placed as it were in effigy.

'On each side of an immense chimney, were suspended the portraits of the first seneschal of Poitou (the illegitimate son of Foulques Taillefer) and his wife Isabella de Lusignan; the progenitors of the grim race of Foulquerres that frowned around. They had the look of being perfect likenesses; and as I gazed on them, I fancied I could trace in their antiquated features some family resemblance to their unfortunate descendant, whom I had slain. This was a dismal neighbourhood, yet the armoury was the only part of the castle that had a habitable air; so I asked the warder whether he could not make a fire, and give me something for supper there, and prepare me a bed in one corner.

'"A fire and a supper you shall have, and that cheerfully, most worthy pilgrim," said he; "but as to a bed, I advise you to come and sleep in my chamber."

'"Why so?" inquired I; "why shall I not sleep in this hall?"

'"I have my reasons; I will make a bed for you close to mine."

'I made no objections, for I recollected that it was Friday, and I dreaded the return of my vision. He brought in billets of wood, kindled a fire in the great overhanging chimney, and then went forth to prepare my supper. I drew a heavy chair before the fire, and seating myself in it, gazed musingly round upon the portraits of the Foulquerres, and the antiquated armour and weapons, the mementos of many a bloody deed. As the day declined, the smoky draperies of the hall gradually became confounded with the dark ground of the paintings, and the lurid gleams from the chimney only enabled me to see visages staring at me from the gathering darkness. All this was dismal in the extreme, and somewhat appalling: perhaps it was the state of my conscience that rendered me particularly sensitive, and prone to fearful imaginings.

'At length the warder brought in my supper. It consisted of a dish of trout, and some crawfish taken in the fosse of the castle. He procured also a bottle of wine, which he informed me was wine of Poitou. I requested him to invite the hermit to join me in my repast; but the holy man sent back word that he allowed himself nothing but roots and herbs, cooked with water. I took my meal, therefore, alone, but prolonged it as much as possible, and sought to cheer my drooping spirits by the wine of Poitou, which I found very tolerable.

'When supper was over, I prepared for my evening devotions. I have always been very punctual in reciting my breviary; it is the prescribed and bounden duty of all cavaliers of the religious orders; and I can answer for it, is faithfully performed by those of Spain. I accordingly drew forth from my pocket a small missal and a rosary, and told the warder he need only designate to me the way to his chamber, where I could come and rejoin him, when I had finished my prayers.

'He accordingly pointed out a winding staircase, opening from the hall. "You will descend this staircase," said he, "until you come to the fourth landing-place, where you enter a vaulted passage, terminated by an arcade, with a statue of the blessed Jeanne of France: you cannot help finding my room, the door of which I will leave open: it is the sixth door from the landing-place. I advise you not to remain in this hall after midnight. Before that hour, you will hear the hermit ring the bell, in going the rounds of the corridors. Do not linger here after that signal."

'The warder retired, and I commenced my devotions. I continued at them earnestly; pausing from time to time to put wood upon the fire. I did not dare to look much around me, for I felt myself becoming a prey to fearful fancies. The pictures appeared to become animated. If I regarded one attentively, for any length of time, it seemed to move the eyes and lips. Above all, the portraits of the Grand Seneschal and his lady, which hung on each side of the great chimney, the progenitors of the Foulquerres of Têtefoulques, regarded me, I thought, with angry and baleful eyes: I even fancied they exchanged significant glances with each other. Just then a terrible blast of wind shook all the casements, and, rushing through the hall, made a fearful rattling and clashing among the armour. To my startled fancy, it seemed something supernatural.

'At length I heard the bell of the hermit, and hastened to quit the hall. Taking a solitary light, which stood on the upper table, I descended the winding staircase; but before I had reached the vaulted passage, leading to the statue of the blessed Jeanne of France, a blast of wind extinguished my taper. I hastily remounted the stairs, to light it again at the chimney; but judge of my feelings, when, on arriving at the entrace to the armoury, I beheld the Seneschal and his lady, who had descended from their frames, and seated themselves on each side of the fireplace!

' "Madam, my love," said the Seneschal, with great formality, and in antiquated phrase, "what think you of the presumption of this Castilian, who comes to harbour himself and make wassail in this our castle, after having slain our descendant, the commander, and that without granting him time for confession?"

' "Truly, my lord," answered the female spectre, with no less stateliness of manner, and with great asperity of tone—"truly, my lord, I opine that this Castilian did a grievous wrong in this encounter; and he should never be suffered to depart hence, without your throwing him the gauntlet." I paused to hear no more, but rushed again down stairs, to seek the chamber of the warder. It was impossible to find it in the darkness, and in the perturbation of my mind. After an hour and a half of fruitless search, and mortal horror and anxieties, I endeavoured to persuade myself that the day was about to break, and listened impatiently for the crowing of the cock; for I thought if I could hear his cheerful note, I should be reassured; catching, in the disordered state of my nerves, at the popular notion that ghosts never appear after the first crowing of the cock.

'At length I rallied myself, and endeavoured to shake off the vague terrors which haunted me. I tried to persuade myself that the two figures which I had seemed to see and hear, had existed only in my troubled imagination. I still had the end of a candle in my hand, and determined to make another effort to relight it, and find my way to bed; for I was ready to sink with fatigue. I accordingly sprang up the staircase, three steps at a time, stopped at the door of the armoury, and peeped cautiously in. The two Gothic figures were no longer in the chimney corners, but I neglected to notice whether they had re-ascended to their frames. I entered, and made desperately for the fire-place, but scarce had I advanced three strides, when Messire Foulques Taillefer stood before me, in the centre of the hall, armed cap-à-pie, and standing in guard, with the point of his sword silently presented to me. I would have retreated to the staircase, but the door of it was occupied by the phantom figure of an esquire, who rudely flung a gauntlet in my face. Driven to fury, I snatched down a sword from the wall: by chance, it was that of the commander which I had placed there. I rushed upon my phantastic adversary, and seemed to pierce him through and through; but at the same time I felt as if something pierced my heart, burning like a red-hot iron. My blood inundated the hall, and I fell senseless.

'When I recovered consciousness, it was broad day, and I found myself in a small chamber, attended by the warder and the hermit. The former told me that on the previous night, he had awakened long after the midnight hour, and perceiving that I had not come to his chamber, he had furnished himself with a vase of holy water, and set out to seek me. He found me stretched senseless on the pavement of the armoury, and bore me to his room. I spoke of my wound; and of the quantity of blood that I had lost. He shook his head, and knew nothing about it; and to my surprise, on examination, I found myself perfectly sound and unharmed. The wound and blood, therefore, had been all delusion. Neither the warder nor the hermit put any questions to me, but advised me to leave the castle as soon as possible. I lost no time in complying with their counsel, and felt my heart relieved from an oppressive weight as I left the gloomy and fate-bound battlements of Têtefoulques behind me.

'I arrived at Bayonne, on my way to Spain, on the following Friday. At midnight I was startled from my sleep, as I had formerly been; but it was no longer by the vision of the dying commander. It was old Foulques Taillefer who stood before me, armed cap-à-pie, and presenting the point of his sword. I made the sign of the cross, and the spectre vanished, but I received the same red-hot thrust in the heart which I had felt in the armoury, and I seemed to be bathed in blood. I would have called out, or have risen from my bed and gone in quest of succour, but I could neither speak nor stir. This agony endured until the crowing of the cock, when I fell asleep again; but the next day I was ill, and in a most pitiable state. I have continued to be harassed by the same vision every Friday night; no acts of penitence and devotion have been able to relieve me from it; and it is only a lingering hope in divine mercy that sustains me, and enables me to support so lamentable a visitation.'

The Grand Prior of Minorca gradually wasted away under constant remorse of conscience, and this horrible incubus. He died some time after, having revealed the preceding particulars of his case, evidently the victim of a diseased imagination.

The above relation has been rendered, in many parts literally, from the French memoir, in which it is given as a true story: if so, it is one of those instances in which truth is more romantic than fiction.

from *Wolfert's Roost*

LEGEND OF THE TWO DISCREET STATUES

There lived once in a waste apartment of the Alhambra a merry little fellow, named Lope Sanchez, who worked in the gardens, and was as brisk and blithe as a grasshopper, singing all day long. He was the life and soul of the fortress; when his work was over, he would sit on one of the stone benches of the esplanade, and strum his guitar, and sing long ditties about the Cid, and Bernardo del Carpio, and Fernando del Pulgar, and other Spanish heroes, for the amusement of the old soldiers of the fortress, or would strike up a merrier tune, and set the girls dancing boleros and fandangos.

Like most little men, Lope Sanchez had a strapping buxom dame for a wife, who could almost have put him in her pocket; but he lacked the usual poor man's lot—instead of ten children he had but one. This was a little black-eyed girl about twelve years of age, named Sanchica, who was as merry as himself, and the delight of his heart. She played about him as he worked in the gardens, danced to his guitar as he sat in the shade, and ran as wild as a young fawn about the groves and alleys and ruined halls of the Alhambra.

It was now the eve of the blessed St. John, and the holiday-loving gossips of the Alhambra, men, women, and children, went up at night to the mountain of the sun, which rises above the Generalife, to keep their midsummer vigil on its level summit. It was a bright moonlight night, and all the mountains were grey and silvery, and the city, with its domes and spires, lay in shadows below, and the Vega was like a fairy land, with haunted streams gleaming among its dusky groves. On the highest part of the mountain they lit up a bonfire, according to an old custom of the country handed down from the Moors. The inhabitants of the surrounding country were keeping a similar vigil, and bonfires, here and there in the Vega, and along the folds of the mountains, blazed up palely in the moonlight.

The evening was gaily passed in dancing to the guitar of Lope Sanchez, who was never so joyous as when on a holiday revel of the kind. While the dance was going on, the little Sanchica with some of her playmates sported among the ruins of an Old Moorish fort that crowns the mountain, when, in gathering pebbles in the fosse, she found a small hand curiously carved of jet, the fingers closed, and the thumb firmly clasped upon them. Overjoyed with her good fortune, she ran to her mother with her prize. It immediately became a subject of sage speculation, and was eyed by some with superstitious distrust. 'Throw it away,' said one; 'it's Moorish—depend upon it there's mischief and witchcraft in it.' 'By no means,' said another; 'you may sell it for something to the jewellers of the Zacatin.' In the midst of this discussion an old tawny soldier drew near, who had served in Africa, and was as swarthy as a Moor. He examined the hand with a knowing look. 'I have seen things of this kind,' said he, 'among the Moors of Barbary. It is a great virtue to guard against the evil eye, and all kinds of spells and enchantments. I give you joy, friend Lope; this bodes good luck to your child.'

Upon hearing this, the wife of Lope Sanchez tied the little hand of jet to a riband, and hung it round the neck of her daughter.

The sight of this talisman called up all the favourite superstitions about the Moors. The dance was neglected, and they sat in groups on the ground, telling old legendary tales, handed down from their ancestors. Some of their stories turned upon the wonders of the very mountain upon which they were seated, which is a famous hobgoblin region. One ancient crone gave a long account of the subterranean palace in the bowels of that mountain where Boabdil and all his Moslem court are said to remain enchanted. 'Among yonder ruins,' said she, pointing to some crumbling walls and mounds of earth on a distant part of the mountain, 'there is a deep black pit that goes down, down into the very heart of the mountain. For all the money in Granada I would not look down into it. Once upon a time a poor man of the Alhambra, who tended goats upon this mountain, scrambled down into that pit after a kid that had fallen in. He came out again all wild and staring, and told such things of what he had seen, that every one thought his brain was turned. He raved for a day or two about the hobgoblin Moors that had pursued him in the cavern, and could hardly be persuaded to drive his goats up again to the mountain. He did so at last, but, poor man, he never came down again. The neighbours found his goats browsing about the Moorish ruins, and his hat and mantle lying near the mouth of the pit, but he was never more heard of.'

The little Sanchica listened with breathless attention to this story. She was of a curious nature, and felt immediately a great hankering to peep into this dangerous pit. Stealing away from her companions, she sought the distant ruins, and after groping for some time among them came to a small hollow, or basin, near the brow of the mountain, where it swept steeply down into the valley of the Darro. In the centre of this basin yawned the mouth of the pit. Sanchica ventured to the verge, and peeped in. All was black as pitch, and gave an idea of immeasurable depth. Her blood ran cold; she drew back, then peeped again, then would have run away, then took another peep—the very horror of the thing was delightful to her. At length she rolled a large stone, and pushed it over the brink. For some time it fell in silence; then struck some rocky projection with a violent crash, then rebounded from side to side, rumbling and tumbling, with a noise like thunder, then made a final splash into water, far, far below—and all was again silent.

The silence, however, did not long continue. It seemed as if something had been awakened within this dreary abyss. A murmuring sound gradually rose out of the pit like the hum and buzz of a beehive. It grew louder and louder; there was the confusion of voices as of a distant multitude, together with the faint din of arms, clash of cymbals, and clangour of trumpets, as if some army were marshalling for battle in the very bowels of the mountain.

The child drew off with silent awe, and hastened back to the place where she had left her parents and their companions. All were gone. The bonfire was expiring, and its last wreath of smoke curling up in the moonshine. The distant fires that had blazed along the mountains and in the Vega were all extinguished, and every thing seemed to have sunk to repose. Sanchica called her parents and some of her companions by name, but received no reply. She ran down the side of the mountain, and by the gardens of the Generalife, until she arrived in the alley of trees leading to the Alhambra, when she seated herself on a bench of a woody recess to recover breath. The bell from the watch-tower of the Alhambra tolled midnight. There was a deep tranquillity, as if all nature slept; excepting the low tinkling sound of an unseen stream that ran under the covert of the bushes. The breathing sweetness of the atmosphere was lulling her to sleep, when her eye was caught by something glittering at a distance; and to her surprise she beheld a long cavalcade of Moorish warriors pouring down the mountain side, and along the leafy avenues. Some were armed with lances and shields; others with scimitars and battle-axes, and with polished cuirasses that flashed in the moonbeams. Their horses pranced proudly, and champed upon their bits, but their tramp caused no more sound than if they had been shod with felt; and the riders were all as pale as death. Among them rode a beautiful lady with a crowned head and long golden locks entwined with pearls. The housings of her palfry were of crimson velvet, embroidered with gold, and swept the earth; but she rode all disconsolate, with eyes ever fixed upon the ground.

Then succeeded a train of courtiers, magnificently arrayed in robes and turbans of divers colours, and amidst them, on a cream-coloured charger, rode King Boabdil el Chico, in a royal mantle, covered with jewels, and a crown sparkling with diamonds. The little Sanchica knew him by his yellow beard, and his resemblance to his portrait, which she had often seen in the picture gallery of the Generalife. She gazed in wonder and admiration at this royal pageant, as it passed glistening among the trees; but though she knew these monarchs, and courtiers, and warriors, so pale and silent, were out of the common course of nature, and things of magic and enchantment, yet she looked on with a bold heart, such courage did she derive from the mystic talisman of the hand, which was suspended about her neck.

The cavalcade having passed by, she rose and followed. It continued on to the great gate of justice, which stood wide open; the old invalid sentinels on duty lay on the stone benches of the barbican, buried in profound and apparently charmed sleep, and the phantom pageant swept noiselessly by them with flaunting banner and triumphant state. Sanchica would have followed; but to her surprise she beheld an opening in the earth, within the barbican, leading down beneath the foundations of the tower. She entered for a little distance, and was encouraged to proceed by finding steps rudely hewn in the rock, and a vaulted passage here and there lit up by a silver lamp, which, while it gave light, diffused likewise a grateful fragrance. Venturing on, she came at last to a great hall, wrought out of the heart of the mountain, magnificently furnished in the Moorish style, and lighted up by silver and crystal lamps. Here, on an ottoman, sat an old man in Moorish dress, with a long white beard, nodding and dozing, with a staff in his hand, which seemed ever to be slipping from his grasp; while at a little distance sat a beautiful lady, in ancient Spanish dress, with a coronet all sparkling with diamonds, and her hair entwined with pearls, who was softly playing on a silver lyre. The little Sanchica now recollected a story she had heard among the old people of the Alhambra, concerning a Gothic princess confined in the centre of the mountain by an old Arabian magician, whom she kept bound up in magic sleep by the power of music.

The lady paused with surprise at seeing a mortal in that enchanted hall. 'Is it the eve of the blessed St. John?' said she.

'It is,' replied Sanchica.

'Then for one night the magic charm is suspended. Come hither, child, and fear not. I am a Christian like thyself, though bound here by enchantment. Touch my fetters with the talisman that hangs about thy neck, and for this night I shall be free.'

So saying, she opened her robes and displayed a broad golden band round her waist, and a golden chain that fastened her to the ground. The child hesitated not to apply the little hand of jet to the golden band, and immediately the chain fell to the earth. At the sound the old man woke and began to rub his eyes; but the lady ran her fingers over the chords of the lyre, and again he fell into a slumber, and began to nod, and his staff to falter in his hand. 'Now,' said the lady, 'touch his staff with the talismanic hand of jet.' The child did so, and it fell from his grasp, and he sunk in a deep sleep on the ottoman. The lady gently laid the silver lyre on the ottoman, leaning it against the head of the sleeping magician; then touching the chords until they vibrated in his ear—'O potent spirit of harmony,' said she, 'continue thus to hold his senses in thraldom till the return of day. Now follow me, my child,' continued she, 'and thou shalt behold the Alhambra as it was in the days of its glory, for thou hast a magic talisman that reveals all enchantments.' Sanchica followed the lady in silence. They passed up through the entrance of the cavern into the barbican of the gate of justice, and thence to the Plaza de los Algibes, or esplanade within the fortress. This was all filled with Moorish soldiery, horse and foot, marshalled in squadrons, with banners displayed. There were royal guards also at the portal, and rows of African blacks with drawn scimitars. No one spake a word, and Sanchica passed on fearlessly after her conductor. Her astonishment increased on entering the royal palace, in which she had been reared. The broad moonshine lit up all the halls, and courts, and gardens, almost as brightly as if it were day, but revealed a far different scene from that to which she was accustomed. The walls of the apartments were no longer stained and rent by time. Instead of cobwebs, they were now hung with rich silks of Damascus, and the gildings and arabesque paintings were restored to their original brilliancy and freshness. The halls, instead of being naked and unfurnished, were set out with divans and ottomans of the rarest stuffs, embroidered with pearls, and studded with precious gems; and all the fountains in the courts and gardens were playing.

The kitchens were again in full operation; cooks were busy preparing shadowy dishes, and roasting and boiling the phantoms of pullets and partridges; servants were hurrying to and fro with silver dishes heaped up with dainties, and arranging a delicious banquet. The Court of Lions was thronged with guards, and courtiers, and alfaquis, as in the old times of the Moors; and at the upper end, in the saloon of judgment, sat Boabdil on his throne, surrounded by his court, and swaying a shadowy sceptre for the night. Notwithstanding all this throng and seeming bustle, not a voice nor a footstep was to be heard; nothing interrupted the midnight silence but the splashing of the fountains. The little Sanchica followed her conductress in mute amazement about the palace, until they came to a portal opening to the vaulted passages beneath the great tower of Comares. On each side of the portal sat the figure of a nymph, wrought out of alabaster. Their heads were turned aside, and their regards fixed upon the same spot within the vault. The enchanted lady paused, and beckoned the child to her. 'Here,' said she, 'is a great secret, which I will reveal to thee in reward for thy faith and courage. These discreet statues watch over a treasure hidden in old times by a Moorish king. Tell thy father to search the spot on which their eyes are fixed, and he will find what will make him richer than any man in Granada. Thy innocent hands alone, however, gifted as thou art also with the talisman, can remove the treasure. Bid thy father use it discreetly, and devote a part of it to the performance of daily masses for my deliverance from this unholy enchantment.'

When the lady had spoken these words, she led the child onward to the little garden of Lindaraxa, which is hard by the vault of the statues. The moon trembled upon the waters of the solitary fountain in the centre of the garden, and shed a tender light upon the orange and citron trees. The beautiful lady plucked a branch of myrtle, and wreathed it round the head of the child. 'Let this be a memento,' said she, 'of what I have revealed to thee, and a testimonial of its truth. My hour is come—I must return to the enchanted hall; follow me not, lest evil befall thee—farewell. Remember what I have said, and have masses performed for my deliverance.' So saying, the lady entered a dark passage leading beneath the tower of Comares, and was no longer seen.

The faint crowing of a cock was now heard from the cottages below the Alhambra, in the valley of the Darro, and a pale streak of light began to appear above the eastern mountains. A slight wind arose, there was a sound like the rustling of dry leaves through the courts and corridors, and door after door shut to with a jarring sound.

Sanchica returned to the scenes she had so lately beheld thronged with the shadowy multitude, but Boabdil and his phantom court were gone. The moon shone into empty halls and galleries stripped of their transient splendour, stained and dilapidated by time, and hung with cobwebs. The bat flitted about in the uncertain light, and the frog croaked from the fish-pond.

Sanchica now made the best of her way to a remote staircase that led up to the humble apartment occupied by her family. The door as usual was open, for Lope Sanchez was too poor to need bolt or bar; she crept quietly to her pallet, and, putting the myrtle wreath beneath her pillow, soon fell asleep.

In the morning she related all that had befallen her to her father. Lope Sanchez, however, treated the whole as a mere dream, and laughed at the child for her credulity. He went forth to his customary labours in the garden, but had not been there long when his little daughter came running to him almost breathless. 'Father! father!' cried she, 'behold the myrtle wreath which the Moorish lady bound round my head.'

Lope Sanchez gazed with astonishment, for the stalk of the myrtle was of pure gold, and every leaf was a sparkling emerald! Being not much accustomed to precious stones, he was ignorant of the real value of the wreath, but he saw enough to convince him that it was something more substantial than the stuff that dreams are generally made of, and that at any rate the child had dreamt to some purpose. His first care was to enjoin the most absolute secrecy upon his daughter; in this respect, however, he was secure, for she had discretion far beyond her years or sex. He then repaired to the vault, where stood the statues of the two alabaster nymphs. He remarked that their heads were turned from the portal, and that the regards of each were fixed upon the same point in the interior of the building. Lope Sanchez could not but admire this most discreet contrivance for guarding a secret. He drew a line from the eyes of the statues to the point of regard, made a private mark on the wall, and then retired.

All day, however, the mind of Lope Sanchez was distracted with a thousand cares. He could not help hovering within distant view of the two statues, and became nervous from the dread that the golden secret might be discovered. Every footstep that approached the place made him tremble. He would have given anything could he but have turned the heads of the statues, forgetting that they had looked precisely in the same direction for some hundreds of years, without any person being the wiser.

'A plague upon them,' he would say to himself, 'they'll betray all; did ever mortal hear of such a mode of guarding a secret?' Then on hearing anyone advance, he would steal off, as though his very lurking near the place would awaken suspicions. Then he would return cautiously, and peep from a distance to see if everything was secure; but the sight of the statues would again call forth his indignation. 'Aye, there they stand,' would he say, 'always looking, and looking, and looking, just where they should not. Confound them! they are just like all their sex; if they have not tongues to battle with, they'll be sure to do it with their eyes.'

At length, to his relief, the long anxious day drew to a close. The sound of footsteps was no longer heard in the echoing halls of the Alhambra; the last stranger passed the threshold, the great portal was barred and bolted, and the bat and the frog, and the hooting owl gradually resumed their nightly vocations in the deserted palace.

Lope Sanchez waited, however, until the night was far advanced before he ventured with his little daughter to the hall of the two nymphs. He found them looking as knowingly and mysteriously as ever at the secret place of deposit. 'By your leaves, gentle ladies,' thought Lope Sanchez, as he passed between them, 'I will relieve you from this charge, that must have set so heavy in your minds for the last two or three centuries.' He accordingly went to work at the part of the wall which he had marked, and in a little while laid open a concealed recess, in which stood two great jars of porcelain. He attempted to draw them forth, but they were immoveable, until touched by the innocent hand of his little daughter. With her aid he dislodged them from their niche, and found, to his great joy, that they were filled with pieces of Moorish gold, mingled with jewels and precious stones. Before daylight he managed to convey them to his chamber, and left the two guardian statues with their eyes still fixed on the vacant wall.

Lope Sanchez had thus on a sudden become a rich man; but riches, as usual, brought a world of cares to which he had hitherto been a stranger. How was he to convey away his wealth with safety? How was he even to enter upon the enjoyment of it without awakening suspicion? Now, too, for the first time in his life the dread of robbers entered into his mind. He looked with terror at the insecurity of his habitation, and went to work to barricado the doors and windows; yet after all his precautions he could not sleep soundly. His usual gaiety was at an end, he had no longer a joke or a song for his neighbours, and, in short, became the most miserable animal in the Alhambra. His old comrades remarked this alteration, pitied him heartily, and began to desert him; thinking he must be falling into want, and in danger of looking to them for assistance. Little did they suspect that his only calamity was riches.

The wife of Lope Sanchez shared his anxiety, but then she had ghostly comfort. We ought before this to have mentioned that Lope, being rather a light inconsiderate little man, his wife was accustomed, in all grave matters, to seek the counsel and ministry of her confessor, Fray Simon, a sturdy broad-shouldered, blue-bearded, bullet-headed friar of the neighbouring convent of San Francisco, who was in fact the spiritual comforter of half the good wives of the neighbourhood. He was moreover in great esteem among divers sisterhoods of nuns; who requited him for his ghostly services by frequent presents of those little dainties and knick-knacks manufactured in convents, such as delicate confections, sweet biscuits, and bottles of spiced cordials, found to be marvellous restoratives after fasts and vigils.

Fray Simon thrived in the exercise of his functions. His oily skin glistened in the sunshine as he toiled up the hill of the Alhambra on a sultry day. Yet notwithstanding his sleek condition, the knotted rope round his waist showed the austerity of his self-discipline; the multitude doffed their caps to him as a mirror of piety, and even the dogs scented the odour of sanctity that exhaled from his garments, and howled from their kennels as he passed.

Such was Fray Simon, the spiritual counsellor of the comely wife of Lope Sanchez; and as the father confessor is the domestic confidant of woman in humble life in Spain, he was soon made acquainted, in great secrecy, with the story of the hidden treasure.

The friar opened eyes and mouth and crossed himself a dozen times at the news. After a moment's pause, 'Daughter of my soul!' said he, 'know that thy husband has committed a double sin—a sin against both state and church! The treasure he hath thus seized upon for himself, being found in the royal domains, belongs of course to the crown; but being infidel wealth, rescued as it were from the very fangs of Satan, should be devoted to the church. Still, however, the matter may be accommodated. Bring hither the myrtle wreath.'

When the good father beheld it, his eyes twinkled more than ever with admiration of the size and beauty of the emeralds. 'This,' said he, 'being the first fruits of this discovery, should be dedicated to pious purposes. I will hang it up as a votive offering before the image of San Francisco in our chapel, and will earnestly pray to him, this very night, that your husband be permitted to remain in quiet possession of your wealth.'

The good dame was delighted to make her peace with heaven

at so cheap a rate, and the friar, putting the wreath under his mantle, departed with saintly steps toward his convent.

When Lope Sanchez came home, his wife told him what had passed. He was excessively provoked, for he lacked his wife's devotion, and had for some time groaned in secret at the domestic visitations of the friar. 'Woman,' said he, 'what hast thou done? thou hast put everything at hazard by thy tattling.'

'What!' cried the good woman, 'would you forbid my disburdening my conscience to my confessor?'

'No, wife! confess as many of your own sins as you please; but as to this money-digging, it is a sin of my own, and my conscience is very easy under the weight of it.'

There was no use, however, in complaining; the secret was told, and, like water spilled on the sand, was not again to be gathered. Their only chance was, that the friar would be discreet.

The next day, while Lope Sanchez was abroad, there was a humble knocking at the door, and Fray Simon entered with meek and demure countenance.

'Daughter,' said he, 'I have prayed earnestly to San Francisco, and he has heard my prayer. In the dead of the night the saint appeared to me in a dream, but with a frowning aspect. "Why," said he, "dost thou pray to me to dispense with this treasure of the Gentiles, when thou seest the poverty of my chapel? Go to the house of Lope Sanchez, crave in my name a portion of the Moorish gold, to furnish two candlesticks for the main altar, and let him possess the residue in peace."'

When the good woman heard of this vision, she crossed herself with awe, and going to the secret place where Lope had hid the treasure, she filled a great leathern purse with pieces of Moorish gold, and gave it to the friar. The pious monk bestowed upon her, in return, benedictions enough, if paid by Heaven, to enrich her race to the latest posterity; then slipping the purse into the sleeve of his habit, he folded his hands upon his breast, and departed with an air of humble thankfulness.

When Lope Sanchez heard of this second donation to the church, he had well nigh lost his senses. 'Unfortunate man,' cried he, 'what will become of me? I shall be robbed by piecemeal; I shall be ruined and brought to beggary!'

It was with the utmost difficulty that his wife could pacify him, by reminding him of the countless wealth that yet remained, and how considerate it was for San Francisco to rest contented with so very small a portion.

Unluckily, Fray Simon had a number of poor relations to be provided for, not to mention some half-dozen sturdy bullet-headed orphan children, and destitute foundlings that he had taken under his care. He repeated his visits, therefore, from day to day, with solicitations on behalf of Saint Dominick, Saint Andrew, Saint James, until poor Lope was driven to despair, and found that, unless he got out of the reach of this holy friar, he should have to make peace offerings to every saint in the calendar. He determined, therefore, to pack up his remaining wealth, beat a secret retreat in the night, and make off to another part of the kingdom.

Full of his project, he bought a stout mule for the purpose, and tethered it in a gloomy vault underneath the tower of the seven floors; the very place from whence the Belludo, or goblin horse, is said to issue forth at midnight, and scour the streets of Granada, pursued by a pack of hell-hounds. Lope Sanchez had little faith in the story, but availed himself of the dread occasioned by it, knowing that no one would be likely to pry into the subterranean stable of the phantom steed. He sent off his family in the course of the day, with orders to wait for him at a distant village of the Vega. As the night advanced, he conveyed his treasure to the vault under the tower, and having loaded his mule, he led it forth, and cautiously descended the dusky avenue.

Honest Lope had taken his measures with the utmost secrecy, imparting them to no one but the faithful wife of his bosom. By some miraculous revelation, however, they became known to Fray Simon. The zealous friar beheld these infidel treasures on the point of slipping for ever out of his grasp, and determined to have one more dash at them for the benefit of the church and San Francisco. Accordingly, when the bells had rung for animas, and all the Alhambra was quiet, he stole out of his convent, and, descending through the gate of justice, concealed himself among the thickets of roses and laurels that border the great avenue. Here he remained, counting the quarters of hours as they were sounded on the bell of the watch tower, and listening to the dreary hootings of owls, and the distant barking of dogs from the gipsy caverns.

At length he heard the tramp of hoofs, and, through the gloom of the overshadowing trees, imperfectly beheld a steed descending the avenue. The sturdy friar chuckled at the idea of the knowing turn he was about to serve honest Lope.

Tucking up the skirts of his habit, and wriggling like a cat watching a mouse, he waited until his prey was directly before him, when darting forth from his leafy covert, and putting one hand on the shoulder and the other on the crupper, he made a vault that would not have disgraced the most experienced master of equitation, and alighted well-forked astride the steed. 'Aha!' said the sturdy friar, 'we shall now see who best understands the game.' He had scarce uttered the words when the mule began to kick, and rear, and plunge, and then set off full speed down the hill. The friar attempted to check him, but in vain. He bounded from rock to rock, and bush to bush; the friar's habit was torn to ribands and fluttered in the wind, his shaven poll received many a hard knock from the branches of the trees, and many a scratch from the brambles. To add to his terror and distress, he found a pack of seven hounds in full cry at his heels, and perceived too late, that he was actually mounted upon the terrible Belludo!

Away then they went, according to the ancient phrase, 'pull devil, pull friar', down the great avenue, across the Plaza Nueva, along the Zacatin, around the Vivarrambla—never did huntsman and hound make a more furious run, or more infernal uproar. In vain did the friar invoke every saint in the calendar, and the holy virgin into the bargain; every time he mentioned a name of the kind it was like a fresh application of the spur, and made the Belludo bound as high as a house. Through the remainder of the night was the unlucky Fray Simon carried

hither and thither, and whither he would not, until every bone
in his body ached, and he suffered a loss of leather too grievous to
be mentioned. At length the crowing of a cock gave the signal of
returning day. At the sound the goblin steed wheeled about, and
gallopped back for his tower. Again he scoured the Vivarrambla,
the Zacatin, the Plaza Nueva, and the avenue of fountains, the
seven dogs yelling, and barking, and leaping up, and snapping
at the heels of the terrified friar. The first streak of day had just
appeared as they reached the tower; here the goblin steed kicked
up his heels, sent the friar a somerset through the air, plunged
into the dark vault followed by the infernal pack, and a
profound silence succeeded to the late deafening clamour.

Was ever so diabolical a trick played off upon a holy friar? A
peasant going to his labours at early dawn found the
unfortunate Fray Simon lying under a fig-tree at the foot of the
tower, but so bruised and bedevilled that he could neither speak
nor move. He was conveyed with all care and tenderness to his
cell, and the story went that he had been waylaid and
maltreated by robbers. A day or two elapsed before he recovered
the use of his limbs; he consoled himself, in the meantime, with
the thoughts, that though the mule with the treasure had
escaped him, he had previously had some rare pickings at the
infidel spoils. His first care on being able to use his limbs, was to
search beneath his pallet, where he had secreted the myrtle
wreath and the leathern pouches of gold extracted from the
piety of dame Sanchez. What was his dismay at finding the
wreath, in effect, but a withered branch of myrtle, and the
leathern pouches filled with sand and gravel!

Fray Simon, with all his chagrin, had the discretion to hold
his tongue; for to betray the secret might draw on him the ridicule
of the public, and the punishment of his superior: it was not until
many years afterwards, on his death-bed, that he revealed to his
confessor his nocturnal ride on the Belludo.

Nothing was heard of Lope Sanchez for a long time after his
disappearance from the Alhambra. His memory was always
cherished as that of a merry companion, though it was feared,
from the care and melancholy observed in his conduct shortly

before his mysterious departure, that poverty and distress had driven him to some extremity. Some years afterwards one of his old companions, an invalid soldier, being at Malaga, was knocked down and nearly run over by a coach and six. The carriage stopped; an old gentleman magnificently dressed, with a bag wig and sword, stepped out to assist the poor invalid. What was the astonishment of the latter to behold in this grand cavalier his old friend Lope Sanchez, who was actually celebrating the marriage of his daughter Sanchica with one of the first grandees in the land.

The carriage contained the bridal party. There was dame Sanchez, now grown as round as a barrel, and dressed out with feathers and jewels, and necklaces of pearls, and necklaces of diamonds, and rings on every finger, and altogether a finery of apparel that had not been seen since the days of Queen Sheba. The little Sanchica had now grown to be a woman, and for grace and beauty might have been mistaken for a duchess, if not a princess outright. The bridegroom sat beside her—rather a withered, spindle-shanked little man, but this only proved him to be of the true blue blood, a legitimate Spanish grandee being rarely above three cubits in stature. The match had been of the mother's making.

Riches had not spoiled the heart of honest Lope. He kept his old comrade with him for several days; feasted him like a king, took him to plays and bull-fights, and at length sent him away rejoicing, with a big bag of money for himself, and another to be distributed among his ancient messmates of the Alhambra.

Lope always gave out that a rich brother had died in America and left him heir to a copper mine; but the shrewd gossips of the Alhambra insist that his wealth was all derived from his having discovered the secret guarded by the two marble nymphs of the Alhambra. It is remarked that these very discreet statues continue, even unto the present day, with their eyes fixed most significantly on the same part of the wall; which leads many to suppose there is still some hidden treasure remaining there well worthy the attention of the enterprising traveller. Though others, and particularly all female visitors, regard them with great complacency as lasting monuments of the fact that women can keep a secret.

from *The Alhambra*

THE ADVENTURES OF THE GERMAN STUDENT

On a stormy night, in the tempestuous times of the French Revolution, a young German was returning to his lodgings, at a late hour, across the old part of Paris. The lightning gleamed, and the loud claps of thunder rattled through the lofty, narrow streets—but I should first tell you something about this young German.

Gottfried Wolfgang was a young man of good family. He had studied for some time at Göttingen, but being of a visionary and enthusiastic character, he had wandered into those wild and speculative doctrines which have so often bewildered German students. His secluded life, his intense application, and the singular nature of his studies, had an effect on both mind and body. His health was impaired; his imagination diseased. He had been indulging in fanciful speculation on spiritual essences until, like Swedenborg, he had an ideal world of his own around him. He took up a notion, I do not know from what cause, that there was an evil influence hanging over him; an evil genius or spirit seeking to ensnare him and ensure his perdition. Such an idea working on his melancholy temperament produced the most gloomy effects. He became haggard and desponding. His friends discovered the mental malady that was preying upon him, and determined that the best cure was a change of scene; he was sent, therefore, to finish his studies amidst the splendours and gaieties of Paris.

Wolfgang arrived at Paris at the breaking out of the

Revolution. The popular delirium at first caught his enthusiastic mind, and he was captivated by the political and philosophical theories of the day: but the scenes of blood which followed shocked his sensitive nature; disgusted him with society and the world, and made him more than ever a recluse. He shut himself up in a solitary apartment in the *Pays Latin*, the quarter of students. There in a gloomy street not far from the monastic walls of the Sorbonne, he pursued his favourite speculations. Sometimes he spent hours together in the great libraries of Paris, those catacombs of departed authors, rummaging among their hoards of dusty and obsolete works in quest of food for his unhealthy appetite. He was, in a manner, a literary ghoul, feeding in the charnel-house of decayed literature.

Wolfgang, though solitary and recluse, was of an ardent temperament, but for a time it operated merely upon his imagination. He was too shy and ignorant of the world to make any advances to the fair, but he was a passionate admirer of female beauty, and in his lonely chamber would often lose himself in reveries on forms and faces which he had seen, and his fancy would deck out images of loveliness far surpassing the reality.

While his mind was in this excited and sublimated state, he had a dream which produced an extraordinary effect upon him. It was of a female face of transcendent beauty. So strong was the impression it made, that he dreamt of it again and again. It haunted his thoughts by day, his slumbers by night; in fine he became passionately enamoured of this shadow of a dream. This lasted so long, that it became one of those fixed ideas which haunt the minds of melancholy men, and are at times mistaken for madness.

Such was Gottfried Wolfgang, and such his situation at the time I mentioned. He was returning home late one stormy night, through some of the old and gloomy streets of the *Marais*, the ancient part of Paris. The loud claps of thunder rattled among the high houses of the narrow streets. He came to the Place de Grève, the square where public executions are performed. The lightning quivered about the pinnacles of the ancient Hôtel de

Ville, and shed flickering gleams over the open space in front. As Wolfgang was crossing the square, he shrunk back with horror at finding himself close by the guillotine. It was the height of the reign of terror, when this dreadful instrument of death stood ever ready, and its scaffold was continually running with blood of the virtuous and the brave. It had that very day been actively employed in the work of carnage, and there it stood in grim array amidst a silent and sleeping city, waiting for fresh victims.

Wolfgang's heart sickened within him, and he was turning shuddering from the horrible engine, when he beheld a shadowy form cowering as it were at the foot of the steps which led up to the scaffold. A succession of vivid flashes of lighting revealed it more distinctly. It was a female figure, dressed in black. She was seated on one of the lower steps of the scaffold, leaning forward, her face hid in her lap, and her long dishevelled tresses hanging to the ground, streaming with the rain which fell in torrents. Wolfgang paused. There was something awful in this solitary monument of woe. The female had the appearance of being above the common order. He knew the times to be full of vicissitude, and that many a fair head, which had once been pillowed on down, now wandered houseless. Perhaps this was some poor mourner whom the dreadful axe had rendered desolate, and who sat here heartbroken on the strand of existence, from which all that was dear to her had been launched into eternity.

He approached, and addressed her in the accents of sympathy. She raised her head and gazed wildly at him. What was his astonishment at beholding, by the bright glare of the lightning, the very face which had haunted him in his dreams. It was pale and disconsolate, but ravishingly beautiful.

Trembling with violent and conflicting emotions, Wolfgang again accosted her. He spoke something of her being exposed at such an hour of the night, and to the fury of such a storm, and offered to conduct her to her friends. She pointed to the guillotine with a gesture of dreadful signification.

'I have no friends on earth!' said she.

'But you have a home,' said Wolfgang.

'Yes—in the grave!'

The heart of the student melted at the words.

'If a stranger dare make an offer,' said he, 'without danger of being misunderstood, I would offer my humble dwelling as a shelter; myself as a devoted friend. I am friendless myself in Paris, and a stranger in the land; but if my life could be of service, it is at your disposal, and should be sacrificed before harm or indignity should come to you.'

There was an honest earnestness in the young man's manner that had its effect. His foreign accent, too, was in his favour; it showed him not to be a hackneyed inhabitant of Paris. Indeed there is an eloquence in true enthusiasm that is not to be doubted. The homeless stranger confided herself implicitly to the protection of the student.

He supported her faltering steps across the Pont Neuf, and by the place where the statue of Henry the Fourth had been overthrown by the populace. The storm had abated, and the thunder rumbled at a distance. All Paris was quiet; that great volcano of human passion slumbered for a while, to gather fresh strength for the next day's eruption. The student conducted his charge through the ancient streets of the *Pays Latin*, and by the dusky walls of the Sorbonne to the great, dingy hotel which he inhabited. The old portress who admitted them stared with surprise at the unusual sight of the melancholy Wolfgang with a female companion.

On entering his apartment, the student, for the first time, blushed at the scantiness and indifference of his dwelling. He had but one chamber—an old fashioned saloon—heavily carved and fantastically furnished with the remains of former magnificence, for it was one of those hotels in the quarter of Luxembourg Palace which had once belonged to nobility. It was lumbered with books and papers, and all the usual apparatus of a student, and his bed stood in a recess at one end.

When lights were brought, and Wolfgang had a better opportunity of contemplating the stranger, he was more than ever intoxicated by her beauty. Her face was pale, but of a dazzling fairness, set off by a profusion of raven hair that hung clustering about it. Her eyes were large and brilliant, with a singular expression that approached almost to wildness. As far as her black dress permitted her shape to be seen, it was of perfect symmetry. Her whole appearance was highly striking, though she was dressed in the simplest style. The only thing approaching to an ornament which she wore was a broad, black band round her neck, clasped by diamonds.

The perplexity now commenced with the student how to dispose of the helpless being thus thrown upon his protection. He thought of abandoning his chamber to her, and seeking shelter for himself elsewhere. Still he was so fascinated by her charms, there seemed to be such a spell upon his thoughts and senses, that he could not tear himself from her presence. Her manner, too, was singular and unaccountable. She spoke no more of the guillotine. Her grief had abated. The attentions of the student had first won her confidence, and then, apparently, her heart. She was evidently an enthusiast like himself, and enthusiasts soon understand each other.

In the infatuation of the moment Wolfgang avowed his passion for her. He told her the story of his mysterious dream, and how she had possessed his heart before he had ever seen her. She was strangely affected by his recital, and acknowledged to have felt an impulse towards him equally unaccountable. It was the time for wild theory and wild actions. Old prejudices and superstitions were done away; everything was under the sway of the 'Goddess of reason.' Among other rubbish of the old times, the forms and ceremonies of marriage began to be considered superfluous binds for honourable minds. Social compacts were the vogue. Wolfgang was too much of a theorist not to be tainted by the liberal doctrines of the day.

'Why should we separate?' said he: 'our hearts are united; in the eye of reason and honour we are as one. What need is there of sordid forms to bind high souls together?'

The stranger listened with emotion: she had evidently received illumination at the same school.

'You have no home nor family,' continued he: 'let me be every thing to you, or rather let us be everything to one another. If form is necessary, form shall be observed—there is my hand. I pledge myself to you forever.'

'For ever?' said the stranger, solemnly.

'For ever!' repeated Wolfgang.

The stranger clasped the hand extended to her: 'Then I am yours,' murmured she, and sunk upon his bosom.

The next morning the student left his bride sleeping, and sallied forth at an early hour to seek more spacious apartments, suitable to the change in his situation. When he returned, he found the stranger lying with her head hanging over the bed, and one arm thrown over it. He spoke to her, but received no reply. He advanced to awaken her from her uneasy posture. On taking her hand, it was cold—there was no pulsation—her face was pallid and ghastly. In a word—she was a corpse.

Horrified and frantic, he alarmed the house. A scene of confusion ensued. The police were summoned. As the officer of police entered the room, he started back on beholding the corpse.

'Great heaven!' cried he, 'how did this woman come here?'

'Do you know any thing about her?' said Wolfgang eagerly.

'Do I?' exclaimed the police officer: 'she was guillotined yesterday!'

He stepped forward; undid the black collar round the neck of the corpse, and the head rolled on the floor!

The student burst into a frenzy. 'The fiend! the fiend has gained possession of me!' shrieked he: 'I am lost for ever!'

They tried to soothe him, but in vain. He was possessed with the frightful belief that an evil spirit had reanimated the dead body to ensnare him. He went distracted, and died in a madhouse.

Here the old gentleman with the haunted head finished his narrative.

'And is this really a fact?' said the inquisitive gentleman.

'A fact not to be doubted,' replied the other. 'I had it from the best authority. The student told it to me himself. I saw him in a madhouse at Paris.*

*The latter part of the above story is founded on an anecdote related to me, and said to exist in print in French. I have not met with it in print.

from *Tales of a Traveller*

THE PHANTOM ISLAND

Break, Phantsie, from thy cave of cloud,
  And wave thy purple wings,
Now all thy figures are allowed,
  And various shapes of things.
Create of airy forms a stream;
  It must have blood and naught of phlegm;
And though it be a walking dream,
  Yet let it like an odour rise
To all the senses here,
  And fall like sleep upon their eyes,
Or music on their ear.

Ben Jonson.

'There are more things in heaven and earth than are dreamed of in our philosophy,' and among these may be placed that marvel and mystery of the seas, the Island of St. Brandan. Those who have read the history of the Canaries, the Fortunate Islands of the ancients, may remember the wonders told of this enigmatical island. Occasionally it would be visible from their shores, stretching away in a clear bright west, to all appearance substantial like themselves, and still more beautiful. Expeditions would launch forth from the Canaries to explore this land of promise. For a time its sun-gilt peaks, and long, shadowy promontories would remain distinctly visible, but in proportion as the voyagers approached, peak and promontory would gradually fade away until nothing would remain but blue sky above and deep blue water below. Hence this mysterious isle was stigmatized by ancient cosmographers with the name of Aprositus, or the Inaccessible. The failure of numerous expeditions sent in quest of it, both in ancient and modern days, have at length caused its very existence to be called in question, and it has been rashly pronounced a mere optical illusion, like the Fata Morgana of the Straits of Messina, or has been classed with those unsubstantial regions known to mariners as Cape Flyaway and the coast of Cloud Land.

Let us not permit, however, the doubts of worldly-wise sceptics to rob us of all the glorious realms owned by happy credulity in days of yore. Be assured, O reader of easy faith!—thou for whom it is my delight to labour—be assured that such an island actually exists, and has, from time to time, been revealed to the gaze and trodden by the feet of favoured mortals. Historians and philosophers may have their doubts, but its existence has been attested by that inspired race, the poets; who, being gifted with a kind of second sight, are enabled to discern those mysteries of nature hidden from the eyes of ordinary men. To this gifted race it has ever been a kind of wonderland. Here once bloomed, and perhaps still blooms, the famous garden of the Hesperides, with its golden fruit. Here too the sorceress Armida had her enchanted garden, in which she held the Christian paladin, Rinaldo, in delicious but inglorious thraldom, as set forth in the immortal lay of Tasso. It was in this island that Sycorax, the witch, held sway, when the good Prospero and his infant daughter, Miranda, were wafted to its shores. Who does not know the tale as told in the magic page of Shakespeare? The island was then—

> . . . *"full of noises,*
> *Sounds, and sweet airs, that give delight, and hurt not."*

The island, in fact, at different times, has been under the sway of different powers, genii of earth, and air, and ocean, who have made it their shadowy abode. Hither have retired many classic but broken-down deities, shorn of almost all their attributes, but who once ruled the poetic world. Here Neptune and Amphitrite hold a diminished court, sovereigns in exile. Their ocean chariot, almost a wreck, lies bottom upward in some sea-beaten cavern: their pursy Tritons and haggard Nereids bask listlessly like seals about the rocks. Sometimes those deities assume, it is said, a shadow of their ancient pomp, and glide in state about a summer sea; and then, as some tall Indiaman lies becalmed with idly flapping sail, her drowsy crew may hear the mellow note of the Triton's shell swelling upon the ear as the invisible pageant sweeps by.

On the shore of this wondrous isle the kraken heaves its unwieldy bulk and wallows many a rood. Here the sea-serpent, that mighty but much contested reptile, lies coiled up during the intervals of its revelations to the eyes of true believers. Here even the Flying Dutchman finds a port, and casts his anchor, and furls his shadowy sail, and takes a brief repose from his eternal cruisings.

In the deep bays and harbours of the island lies many a spell-bound ship, long since given up as lost by the ruined merchant. Here, too, its crew, long, long bewailed in vain, lie sleeping from age to age, in mossy grottoes, or wander about in pleasing oblivion of all things. Here in caverns are garnered the priceless treasures lost in the ocean. Here sparkles in vain the diamond and flames the carbuncle. Here are piled up rich bales of Oriental silks, boxes of pearls, and piles of golden ingots.

Such are some of the marvels related of this island, which may serve to throw light upon the following legend, of unquestionable truth, which I recommend to the implicit belief of the reader.

THE ADELANTADO OF THE SEVEN CITIES

A legend of St. Brandan

In the early part of the fifteenth century, when Prince Henry of Portugal, of worthy memory, was pushing the career of discovery along the western coast of Africa, and the world was resounding with reports of golden regions on the mainland, and new-found islands in the ocean, there arrived at Lisbon an old bewildered pilot of the seas, who had been driven by tempests, he knew not whither, and roved about an island far in the deep, upon which he had landed, and which he had found peopled with Christians, and adorned with noble cities.

The inhabitants, he said, having never before been visited by a ship, gathered round, and regarded him with surprise. They told him they were descendants of a band of Christians, who fled from Spain when that country was conquered by the Moslems. They were curious about the state of their fatherland, and grieved to hear that the Moslems still held possession of the kingdom of Granada. They would have taken the old navigator to church, to convince him of their orthodoxy; but, either through lack of devotion, or lack of faith in their words, he declined their invitation, and preferred to return on board of his ship. He was properly punished. A furious storm arose, drove him from his anchorage, hurried him out to sea, and he saw no more of the unknown island.

This strange story caused a great marvel in Lisbon and elsewhere. Those versed in history remembered to have read, in an ancient chronicle, that, at the time of the conquest of Spain, in the eighth century, when the blessed cross was cast down, and the crescent erected in its place, and when Christian churches were turned into Moslem mosques, seven bishops, at the head of seven bands of pious exiles, had fled from the peninsula, and embarked in quest of some ocean island, or distant land, where they might found seven Christian cities, and enjoy their faith unmolested.

The fate of these saints-errant had hitherto remained a mystery, and their story had faded from memory; the report of the old tempest-tossed pilot, however, revived this long-forgotten theme; and it was determined by the pious and enthusiastic, that the island thus accidentally discovered, was the identical place of refuge, whither the wandering bishops had been guided by a protecting Providence, and where they had folded their flocks.

This most excitable of worlds has always some darling object of chimerical enterprise; the 'Island of the Seven Cities' now awakened as much interest and longing among zealous Christians, as has the renowned city of Timbuctoo among adventurous travellers, or the North East passage among hardy navigators; and it was a frequent prayer of the devout, that these scattered and lost portions of the Christian family might be discovered, and reunited to the great body of Christendom.

No one, however, entered into the matter with half the zeal of Don Fernando de Ulmo, a young cavalier, of high standing in the Portuguese court, and of most sanguine and romantic temperament. He had recently come to his estate, and had run the round of all kinds of pleasures and excitements, when this new theme of popular talk and wonder presented itself. The Island of the Seven Cities became now the constant subject of his thoughts by day, and his dreams by night: it even rivalled his passion for a beautiful girl, one of the greatest belles of Lisbon, to whom he was betrothed. At length, his imagination became so inflamed on the subject, that he determined to fit out an expedition, at his own expense, and set sail in quest of this sainted island. It could not be a cruise of any great extent; for, according to the calculations of the tempest-tossed pilot, it must be somewhere in the latitude of the Canaries; which at that time, when the new world was yet undiscovered, formed the frontier of ocean enterprise. Don Fernando applied to the Crown for countenance and protection. As he was a favourite at court, the usual patronage was readily extended to him; that is to say, he received a commission from the king, Don Joam II, constituting him Adelantado, or military governor, of any country he might discover, with the single proviso, that he should bear all the expenses of the discovery, and pay a tenth of the profits to the crown.

Don Fernando now set to work in the true spirit of a projector. He sold acre after acre of solid land, and invested the proceeds in ships, guns, ammunition, and sea-stores. Even his old family mansion, in Lisbon, was mortgaged without scruple, for he looked forward to a palace in one of the Seven Cities, of which he was to be Adelantado. This was the age of nautical romance, when the thoughts of all speculative dreamers were turned to the ocean. The scheme of Don Fernando, therefore, drew adventurers of every kind. The merchant promised himself new marts of opulent traffic; the soldier hoped to sack and plunder some one or other of those Seven Cities; even the fat monk shook off the sleep and sloth of the cloister, to join in a crusade which promised such increase to the possessions of the church.

One person alone regarded the whole project with sovereign contempt and growling hostility. This was Don Ramiro Alvarez, the father of the beautiful Serafina, to whom Don Fernando was betrothed. He was one of those perverse, matter-of-fact old men, who are prone to oppose every thing speculative and romantic. He had no faith in the Island of the Seven Cities; regarded the projected cruise as a crack-brained freak; looked with angry eye and internal heart-burning on the conduct of his intended son-in-law, chaffering away solid lands for lands in the moon; and scoffingly dubbed him Adelantado of Cloud Land. In fact, he had never really relished the intended match, to which his consent had been slowly extorted, by the tears and entreaties of his daughter. It is true he could have no reasonable objections to the youth, for Don Fernando was the very flower of Portuguese chivalry. No one could excel him at the tilting-match, or the riding at the ring; none was more bold and dexterous in the bullfight; none composed more gallant madrigals in praise of his lady's charms, or sang them with sweeter tones to the accompaniment of her guitar; nor could any one handle the castanets and dance the bolero with more captivating grace. All these admirable qualities and endowments, however, though they had been sufficient to win the heart of Serafina, were nothing in the eyes of her unreasonable father. O Cupid, god of Love! why will fathers always be so unreasonable?

The engagement to Serafina had threatened at first to throw an obstacle in the way of the expedition of Don Fernando, and for a time perplexed him in the extreme. He was passionately attached to the young lady; but he was also passionately bent on this romantic enterprise. How should he reconcile the two passionate inclinations? A simple and obvious arrangement at length presented itself: marry Serafina, enjoy a portion of the honeymoon at once, and defer the rest until his return from the discovery of the Seven Cities!

He hastened to make known this most excellent arrangement to Don Ramiro, when the long-smothered wrath of the old cavalier burst forth. He reproached him with being the dupe of wandering vagabonds and wild schemers, and with squandering all his real possessions, in pursuit of empty bubbles. Don Fernando was too sanguine a projector, and too young a man, to listen tamely to such language. He acted with what is technically called 'becoming spirit.' A high quarrel ensued; Don Ramiro pronounced him a madman, and forbade all farther intercourse with his daughter, until he should give proof of returning sanity, by abandoning this madcap enterprise; while Don Fernando flung out of the house, more bent than ever on the expedition, from the idea of triumphing over the incredulity of the greybeard, when he should return successful. Don Ramiro's heart misgave him. Who knows, thought he, but this crack-brained visionary may persuade my daughter to elope with him, and share his throne in this unknown paradise of fools? If only I could keep her safe until his ships are fairly out at sea!

He repaired to her apartment, represented to her the sanguine, unsteady character of her lover, and the chimerical value of his schemes, and urged the propriety of suspending all intercourse with him until he should recover from his hallucination. She bowed her head as if in filial acquiescence, whereupon he folded her to his bosom with parental fondness, and kissed away a tear that was stealing over her cheek, but as he left the chamber, quietly turned the key in the lock; for though he was a fond father, and had a high opinion of the submissive temper of his child, he had a still higher opinion of the conservative virtues of lock and key, and determined to trust to them until the caravels should sail. Whether the damsel had been in any wise shaken in her faith as to the schemes of her lover by her father's eloquence, tradition does not say; but certain it is, that, the moment she heard the key turn in the lock, she became a firm believer in the Island of the Seven Cities.

The door was locked; but her will was unconfined. A window of the chamber opened into one of those stone balconies, secured by iron bars, which project like huge cages from Portuguese and Spanish houses. Within this balcony the beautiful Serafina had her birds and flowers, and here she was accustomed to sit on moonlight nights as in a bower, and touch her guitar and sing like a wakeful nightingale. From this balcony an intercourse was now maintained between the lovers, against which the lock and key of Don Ramiro were of no avail. All day would Fernando be occupied hurrying the equipment of his ships, but evening found him in sweet discourse beneath his lady's window.

At length the preparations were completed. Two gallant caravels lay at anchor in the Tagus ready to sail at sunrise. Late at night by the pale light of a waning moon the lover had his last interview. The beautiful Serafina was sad at heart and full of dark forebodings; her lover full of hope and confidence. 'A few short months,' said he, 'and I shall return in triumph. Thy father will then blush at his incredulity, and hasten to welcome to his house the Adelantado of the Seven Cities.'

The gentle lady shook her head. It was not on this point she felt distrust. She was a thorough believer in the Island of the Seven Cities, and so sure of the success of the enterprise, that she might have been tempted to join it had not the balcony been high and the grating strong. Other considerations induced that dubious shaking of the head. She had heard of the inconstancy of the seas, and the inconstancy of those who roam them. Might not Fernando meet with other loves in foreign ports? Might not some peerless beauty in one or other of those Seven Cities efface the image of Serafina from his mind? Now let the truth be spoken, the beautiful Serafina had reason for her disquiet. If Don Fernando had any fault in the world, it was that of being rather inflammable and apt to take fire from every sparkling eye. He had been somewhat of a rover among the sex on shore; what might he be on sea?

She ventured to express her doubt, but he spurned at the very idea. 'What! he false to Serafina! He bow at the shrine of another beauty? Never! never!' Repeatedly did he bend his knee, and smite his breast, and call upon the silver moon to witness his sincerity and truth.

He retorted the doubt, 'Might not Serafina herself forget her plighted faith? Might not some wealthier rival present himself while he was tossing on the sea, and backed by her father's wishes, win the treasure of her hand!'

The beautiful Serafina raised her white arms between the iron bars of the balcony, and, like her lover, invoked the moon to testify her vows. Alas! how little did Fernando know her heart. The more her father should oppose, the more would she be fixed in faith. Though years should intervene, Fernando on his return would find her true. Even should the salt sea swallow him up (and her eyes shed salt tears at the very thought), never would she be the wife of another! Never, *never*, NEVER! She drew from her finger a ring gemmed with a ruby heart, and dropped it from the balcony, a parting pledge of constancy.

Thus the lovers parted, with many a tender word and plighted vow. But will they keep those vows? Perish the doubt! Have they not called the constant moon to witness?

With the morning dawn the caravels dropped down the Tagus, and put to sea. They steered for the Canaries, in those days the regions of nautical discovery and romance, and the outposts of the known world, for as yet Columbus had not steered his daring barks across the ocean. Scarce had they reached those latitudes when they were separated by a violent tempest. For many days was the caravel of Don Fernando driven about at the mercy of the elements; all seamanship was baffled, destruction seemed inevitable, and the crew were in despair. All at once the storm subsided; the ocean sank into a calm; the clouds, which had veiled the face of heaven, were suddenly withdrawn, and the tempest-tossed mariners beheld a fair and mountainous island, emerging as if by enchantment from the murky gloom. They rubbed their eyes, and gazed for a time almost incredulously; yet there lay the island, spread out in lovely landscapes, with the late stormy sea laving its shores with peaceful billows.

The pilot of the caravel consulted his maps and charts; no island like the one before him was laid down as existing in those parts; it is true he had lost his reckoning in the late storm, but, according to his calculations, he could not be far from the Canaries; and this was not one of that group of islands. The caravel now lay perfectly becalmed off the mouth of a river; on the banks of which, about a league from the sea, was descried a noble city, with lofty walls and towers, and a protecting castle.

After a time, a stately barge, with sixteen oars, was seen emerging from the river, and approaching the caravel. It was quaintly carved and gilt; the oarsmen were clad in antique garb, their oars painted of a bright crimson, and they came slowly and solemnly, keeping time as they rowed to the cadence of an old Spanish ditty. Under a silken canopy in the stern, sat a cavalier richly clad, and over his head was a banner bearing the sacred emblem of the cross.

When the barge reached the caravel, the cavalier stepped on board. He was tall and gaunt, with a long Spanish visage, moustaches that curled up to his eyes, and a forked beard. He wore gauntlets reaching to his elbows, a Toledo blade strutting out behind, with a basket hilt, in which he carried his handkerchief. His air was lofty and precise, and bespoke indisputably the hidalgo. Thrusting out a long spindle leg, he took off a huge sombrero, and swaying it until the feather swept the ground, accosted Don Fernando in the old Castilian language and with the old Castilian courtesy, welcoming him to the Island of the Seven Cities.

Don Fernando was overwhelmed with astonishment. Could this be true? Had he really been tempest-driven to the very land of which he was in quest?

It was even so. That very day the inhabitants were holding high festival in commemoration of the escape of their ancestors from the Moors. The arrival of the caravel at such a juncture was considered a good omen, the accomplishment of an ancient prophecy through which the island was to be restored to the great community of Christendom. The cavalier before him was grand-chamberlain, sent by the alcayde to invite him to the festivities of the capital.

Don Fernando could scarce believe that this was not all a dream. He made known his name, and the object of his voyage. The grand-chamberlain declared that all was in perfect accordance with the ancient prophecy, and that the moment that his credentials were presented, he would be acknowledged as the Adelantado of the Seven Cities. In the meantime the day was waning; the barge was ready to convey him to the land, and would as assuredly bring him back.

Don Fernando's pilot, a veteran of the seas, drew him aside, and expostulated against his venturing, on the mere word of a stranger, to land in a strange barge on an unknown shore. 'Who knows, Señor, what land this is, or what people inhabit it?'

Don Fernando was not to be dissuaded. Had he not believed in this island when all the world doubted? Had he not sought it in defiance of storm and tempest, and was he now to shrink from its shores when they lay before him in calm weather? In a word, was not faith the very cornerstone of his enterprise?

Having arrayed himself, therefore, in gala-dress, befitting the occasion, he took his seat in the barge. The grand-chamberlain seated himself opposite. The rowers plied their oars, and renewed the mournful old ditty, and the gorgeous but unwieldy barge moved slowly through the water.

The night closed in before they entered the river, and swept along past rock and promontory, each guarded by its tower. At every post they were challenged by the sentinel.

'Who goes there?'

'The Adelantado of the Seven Cities.'

'Welcome, Señor Adelantado. Pass on.'

Entering the harbour, they rowed close by an armed galley of ancient form. Soldiers with crossbows patrolled the deck.

'Who goes there?'

'The Adelantado of the Seven Cities.'

'Welcome, Señor Adelantado. Pass on.'

They landed at a broad flight of stone steps, leading up between two massive towers, and knocked at the water-gate. A sentinel, in ancient steel casque, looked from the barbican.

'Who is there?'

'The Adelantado of the Seven Cities.'

'Welcome, Señor Adelantado.'

The gate swung open, grating upon rusty hinges. They entered between two rows of warriors in gothic armour, with cross-bows, maces, battle-axes, and faces old-fashioned as their armour. There were processions through the streets, in commemoration of the landing of the seven Bishops and their followers, and bonfires, at which effigies of losel Moors expiated their invasion of Christendom by a kind of *auto-da-fe*. The groups round the fires, uncouth in their attire, looked like the fantastic figures that roam the streets in Carnival time. Even the dames who gazed down from gothic balconies hung with antique tapestry, resembled effigies dressed up in Christmas mummeries. Every thing, in short, bore the stamp of former ages, as if the world had suddenly rolled back for several centuries. Nor was this to be wondered at. Had not the Island of the Seven Cities been cut off from the rest of the world for several hundred years; and were not these the modes and customs of Gothic Spain before it was conquered by the Moors?

Arrived at the palace of the alcayde, the grand-chamberlain knocked at the portal. The porter looked through a wicket, and demanded who was there.

'The Adelantado of the Seven Cities.'

The portal was thrown wide open. The grand-chamberlain led the way up a vast, heavily-moulded, marble staircase, and into a hall of ceremony, where was the alcayde with several of the principle dignitaries of the city, who had a marvellous resemblance, both in form and feature, to the quaint figures in old illuminated manuscripts.

The grand-chamberlain stepped forward and announced the name and title of the stranger guest, and the extraordinary nature of his mission. The announcement appeared to create no extraordinary emotion or surprise, but to be received as the anticipated fulfilment of a prophecy.

The reception of Don Fernando, however, was profoundly gracious, though in the same style of stately courtesy which everywhere prevailed. He would have produced his credentials, but this was courteously declined. The evening was devoted to high festivity; the following day, when he should enter the port with his caravel, would be devoted to business, when the credentials would be received in due form, and he inducted into office as Adelantado of the Seven Cities.

Don Fernando was now conducted through one of those interminable suites of apartments, the pride of Spanish palaces, all furnished in the style of obsolete magnificence. In a vast saloon, blazing with tapers, was assembled all the aristocracy and fashion of the city; stately dames and cavaliers, the very counterpart of the figures in the tapestry which decorated the walls. Fernando gazed in silent marvel. It was a reflex of the proud aristocracy of Spain in the time of Roderick the Goth.

The festivities of the evening were all in the style of solemn and antiquated ceremonial. There was a dance, but it was as if the old tapestry were put in motion, and all the figures moving in stately measures about the floor. There was one exception, and one that told powerfully upon the susceptible Adelantado. The alcayde's daughter—such a ripe, melting beauty! Her dress, it is true, like the dresses of her neighbours, might have been worn before the flood, but she had the black Andalusian eye, a glance of which, through its long dark lashes, is irresistible. Her voice, too, her manner, her undulating movement, all smacked of Andalusia, and showed how female charms may be transmitted from age to age, and clime to clime, without ever going out of fashion. Those who know the witchery of the sex, in that most amorous part of amorous old Spain, may judge of the fascination to which Don Fernando was exposed, as he joined in the dance with one of its most captivating descendants.

He sat beside her at the banquet! such an old-world feast! such obsolete dainties! At the head of the table the peacock, that bird of state and ceremony was served up in full plumage on a golden dish. As Don Fernando cast his eyes down the glittering board, what a vista presented itself of odd heads and head-dresses; of formal bearded dignitaries and stately dames, with castellated locks and towering plumes! Is it to be wondered at that he should turn with delight from these antiquated figures to the alcayde's daughter, all smiles and dimples, and melting looks and melting accents? Beside, for I wish to give him every excuse in my power, he was in a particularly excitable mood from the novelty of the scene before him, from this realization of all his hopes and fancies, and from frequent draughts of the wine cup presented to him at every moment by officious pages during the banquet.

In a word—there is no concealing the matter—before the evening was over, Don Fernando was making love outright to the alcayde's daughter. They had wandered together to a moon-lit balcony of the palace, and he was charming her ear with one of those love ditties with which, in a like balcony, he had serenaded the beautiful Serafina.

The damsel hung her head coyly. 'Ah! Señor, these are flattering words; but you cavaliers, who roam the seas, are unsteady as its waves. Tomorrow you will be throned in state, Adelantado of the Seven Cities; and will think no more of the alcayde's daughter.'

Don Fernando, in the intoxication of the moment, called the moon to witness his sincerity. As he raised his hand in adjuration, the chaste moon cast a ray upon the ring that sparkled on his finger. It caught the damsel's eye. 'Señor

Adelantado,' said she archly, 'I have no great faith in the moon, but give me that ring upon your finger in pledge of the truth of what you profess.'

The gallant Adelantado was taken by surprise; there was no parrying this sudden appeal: before he had time to reflect, the ring of the beautiful Serafina glittered on the finger of the alcayde's daughter.

At this eventful moment the chamberlain approached with lofty demeanour, and announced that the barge was waiting to bear him back to the caravel. I forbear to relate the ceremonious partings with the alcayde and his dignitaries, and the tender farewell of the alcayde's daughter. He took his seat in the barge opposite the grand-chamberlain. The rowers plied their crimson oars in the same stately manner to the cadence of the same mournful old ditty. His brain was in a whirl with all that he had seen, and his heart now and then gave him a twinge as he thought of his temporary infidelity to the beautiful Serafina. The barge sallied out into the sea, but no caravel was to be seen; doubtless she had been carried to a distance by the current of the river. The oarsmen rowed on; their monotonous chant had a lulling effect. A drowsy influence crept over Don Fernando. Objects swam before his eyes. The oarsmen assumed odd shapes as in a dream. The grand-chamberlain grew larger and larger, and taller. He took off his huge sombrero, and held it over the head of Don Fernando, like an extinguisher over a candle. The latter cowered beneath it; he felt himself sinking in the socket.

'Good night, Señor Adelantado of the Seven Cities!' said the grand-chamberlain.

The sombrero slowly descended—Don Fernando was extinguished!

How long he remained extinct no mortal man can tell. When he returned to consciousness, he found himself in a strange cabin, surrounded by strangers. He rubbed his eyes, and looked round him wildly. Where was he?—On board of a Portuguese ship, bound to Lisbon. How came he there?—He had been taken senseless from a wreck drifting about the ocean.

Don Fernando was more and more confounded and

perplexed. He recalled, one by one, every thing that had happened to him in the Island of the Seven Cities, until he had been extinguished by the sombrero of the grand-chamberlain. But what had happened to him since? What had become of his caravel? Was it the wreck of her on which he had been found floating?

The people about him could give no information on the subject. He entreated them to take him to the Island of the Seven Cities, which could not be far off. Told them all that had befallen him there. That he had but to land to be received as Adelantado; when he would reward them magnificently for their services.

They regarded his words as the ravings of delirium, and in their honest solicitude for the restoration of his reason, administered such rough remedies that he was fain to drop the subject and observe a cautious taciturnity.

At length they arrived at the Tagus, and anchored before the famous city of Lisbon. Don Fernando sprang joyfully on shore, and hastened to his ancestral mansion. A strange porter opened the door, who knew nothing of him or of his family; no people of the name had inhabited the house for many a year.

He sought the mansion of Don Ramiro. He approached the balcony beneath which he had bidden farewell to Serafina. Did his eyes deceive him? No! There was Serafina herself among the flowers in the balcony. He raised his arms toward her with an exclamation of rapture. She cast upon him a look of indignation, and, hastily retiring, closed the casement with a slam that testified her displeasure.

Could she have heard of his flirtation with the alcayde's daughter? But that was mere transient gallantry. A moment's interview would dispel every doubt of his constancy.

He rang at the door; as it was opened by the porter he rushed up stairs; sought the well-known chamber, and threw himself at the feet of Serafina. She started back with affright, and took refuge in the arms of a youthful cavalier.

'What mean you, Señor,' cried the latter, 'by this intrusion?'

'What right have you to ask the question?' demanded Don Fernando fiercely.

'The right of an affianced suitor!'

Don Fernando started and turned pale. 'Oh, Serafina! Serafina!' cried he, in a tone of agony; 'is this thy plighted constancy?'

'Serafina? What mean you by Serafina, Señor? If this be the lady you intend, her name is Maria.'

'May I not believe my sense? May I not believe my heart?' cried Don Fernando. Is not this Serafina Alvarez, the original of yon portrait, which, less fickle than herself, still smiles on me from the wall?'

'Holy Virgin!' cried the young lady, casting her eyes upon the portrait. 'He is talking of my great-grandmother!'

An explanation ensued, if that could be called an explanation, which plunged the unfortunate Fernando into tenfold perplexity. If he might believe his eyes, he saw before him his beloved Serafina; if he might believe his ears, it was merely her hereditary form and features, perpetuated in the person of her great-granddaughter.

His brain began to spin. He sought the office of the Minister of Marine, and made a report of his expedition, and of the Island of the Seven Cities, which he had so fortunately discovered. Nobody knew anything of such an expedition, or such an island. He declared that he had undertaken the enterprise under a formal contract with the crown, and had received a regular commission, constituting him Adelantado. This must be matter of record, and he insisted loudly, that the books of the department should be consulted. The wordy strife at length attracted the attention of an old gray-headed clerk, who sat perched on a high stool, at a high desk, with iron-rimmed spectacles on the top of a thin, pinched nose, copying records into an enormous folio. He had wintered and summered in the department for a great part of a century, until he had almost grown to be a piece of the desk at which he sat; his memory was a mere index of official facts and documents, and his brain was little better than red tape and parchment. After peering down for a time from his lofty perch, and ascertaining the matter in controversy, he put his pen behind his ear, and descended. He remembered to have heard something from his predecessor about an expedition of the kind in question, but then it had sailed during the reign of Dom Joam II, and he had been dead at least a hundred years. To put the matter beyond dispute, however, the archives of the Torre do Tombo, that sepulchre of old Portuguese documents, were diligently searched, and a record was found of a contract between the Crown and one Fernando de Ulmo, for the discovery of the Island of the Seven Cities, and of a commission secured to him as Adelantado of the country he might discover.

'There!' cried Don Fernando, triumphantly, 'there you have proof, before your own eyes, of what I have said. I am the Fernando de Ulmo specified in that record. I have discovered the Island of the Seven Cities, and am entitled to be Adelantado, according to contract.'

The story of Don Fernando had certainly, what is pronounced the best of historical foundation, documentary evidence; but when a man, in the bloom of youth, talked of events that had taken place above a century previously, as having happened to himself, it is no wonder that he was set down for a madman.

The old clerk looked at him from above and below his spectacles, shrugged his shoulders, stroked his chin, reascended his lofty stool, took the pen from behind his ear, and resumed his daily and eternal task, copying records into the fiftieth volume of a series of gigantic folios. The other clerks winked at each other shrewdly, and dispersed to their several places, and poor Don Fernando, thus left to himself, flung out of the office, almost driven wild by these repeated perplexities.

In the confusion of his mind, he instinctively repaired to the mansion of Alvarez, but it was barred against him. To break the delusion under which the youth apparently laboured, and to convince him that the Serafina about whom he raved was really dead, he was conducted to her tomb. There she lay, a stately matron, cut out in alabaster; and there lay her husband beside her; a portly cavalier, in armour; and there knelt on each side, the effigies of a numerous progeny, proving that she had been a

fruitful vine. Even the very monument gave evidence of the
lapse of time; the hands of her husband, folded as if in prayer,
had lost their fingers, and the face of the once lovely Serafina was
without a nose.

Don Fernando felt a transient glow of indignation at
beholding this monumental proof of the inconstancy of his
mistress; but who could expect a mistress to remain constant
during a whole century of absence? And what right had he to
rail about constancy, after what had passed between himself and
the alcayde's daughter? The unfortunate cavalier performed
one pious act of tender devotion; he had the alabaster nose of
Serafina restored by a skilful statuary, and then tore himself
from the tomb.

He could no longer doubt the fact that, somehow or other, he
had skipped over a whole century, during the night he had spent
at the Island of the Seven Cities; and he was now as complete a
stranger in his native city as if he had never been there. A
thousand times did he wish himself back to that wonderful
island, with its antiquated banquet halls, where he had been so
courteously received; and now that the once young and
beautiful Serafina was nothing but a great-grandmother in
marble, with generations of descendants, a thousand times
would he recall the melting black eyes of the alcayde's daughter,
who doubtless, like himself, was still flourishing in fresh
juvenility, and breathe a secret wish that he were seated by her
side.

He would at once have set on foot another expedition, at his
own expense, to cruise in search of the sainted island, but his
means were exhausted. He endeavoured to rouse others to the
enterprise, setting forth the certainty of profitable results, of
which his own experience furnished such unquestionable proof.
Alas! no one would give ear to his tale; but looked upon it as the
feverish dream of a shipwrecked man. He persisted in his efforts;
holding forth in all places and all companies, until he became an
object of jest and jeer to the light-minded, who mistook his
earnest enthusiasm for a proof of insanity; and the very children
in the streets bantered him with the title of 'The Adelantado of
the Seven Cities'.

Finding all efforts in vain in his native city of Lisbon, he took shipping for the Canaries, as being nearer the latitude of his former cruise, and inhabited by people given to nautical adventure. Here he found ready listeners to his story; for the old pilots and mariners of those parts were notorious island-hunters and devout believers in all the wonders of the seas. Indeed, one and all treated his adventure as a common occurrence, and turning to each other, with a sagacious nod of the head, observed, 'He had been at the Island of St. Brandan'.

They then went on to inform him of that great marvel and enigma of the ocean; of its repeated appearance to the inhabitants of their islands; and of the many, but ineffectual, expeditions that had been made in search of it. They took him to a promontory of the island of Palma, whence the shadowy St. Brandan had oftenest been descried, and they pointed out the very tract in the west where its mountains had been seen.

Don Fernando listened with rapt attention. He had no longer a doubt that this mysterious and fugacious island must be the same with that of the Seven Cities; and that some supernatural influence connected with it had operated upon himself, and made the events of the night occupy the space of a century.

He endeavoured, but in vain, to rouse the islanders to another attempt at discovery; they had given up the phantom island as indeed inaccessible. Fernando, however was not to be discouraged. The idea wore itself deeper and deeper in his mind, until it became the engrossing subject of his thoughts and the object of his being. Every morning he would repair to the promontory of Palma, and sit there throughout the livelong day, in hopes of seeing the fairy mountains of St. Brandan peering above the horizon; every evening he returned to his home, a disappointed man, but ready to resume his post on the following morning.

His assiduity was all in vain. He grew grey in his ineffectual attempt; and was at length found dead at his post. His grave is still shown in the island of Palma, and a cross is erected on the spot where he used to sit and look out upon the sea, in hopes of the re-appearance of the phantom island.

from *Wolfert's Roost*

GUESTS FROM GIBBET ISLAND

Whoever has visited the ancient and renowned village of Communipaw, may have noticed an old stone building, of most ruinous and sinister appearance. The doors and window-shutters are ready to drop from their hinges; old clothes are stuffed in the broken panes of glass; while legions of half-starved dogs prowl about the premises, and rush out and bark at every passer-by; for your beggarly house in a village is most apt to swarm with profligate and ill-conditioned dogs. What adds to the sinister appearance of this mansion, is a tall frame in front, not a little resembling a gallows, and which looks as if waiting to accommodate some of the inhabitants with a well-merited airing. It is not a gallows, however, but an ancient sign-post; for this dwelling in the golden days of Communipaw, was one of the most orderly and peaceful of village taverns, where public affairs were talked and smoked over. In fact, it was in this very building that Oloffe the Dreamer, and his companions, concerted that great voyage of discovery and colonization, in which they explored Buttermilk Channel, were nearly shipwrecked in the Strait of Hell-gate, and finally landed on the Island of Manhattan, and founded the great city of New Amsterdam.

Even after the province had been cruelly wrested from the sway of their High Mightinesses, by the combined forces of the British and the Yankees, this tavern continued its ancient loyalty. It is true, the head of the Prince of Orange disappeared from the sign, a strange bird being painted over it, with the explanatory legend of *Die Wilde Gans*, or The Wild Goose; but this all the world knew to be a sly riddle of the landlord, the worthy Teunis Van Gieson, a knowing man in a small way, who laid his finger beside his nose and winked, when any one studied the signification of his sign, and observed that his goose was hatching, but would join the flock whenever they flew over the water; an enigma which was the perpetual recreation and delight of the loyal but fat-headed burghers of Communipaw.

Under the sway of this patriotic, though discreet and quiet publican, the tavern continued to flourish in primeval tranquillity, and was the resort of true-hearted Nederlanders, from all parts of Pavonia; who met here quietly and secretly, to smoke and drink the downfall of Briton and Yankee, and success to Admiral Van Tromp.

The only drawback on the comfort of the establishment, was a nephew of mine host, a sister's son, Yan Yost Vanderscamp by name, and a real scamp by nature. This unlucky whipster showed an early propensity to mischief, which he gratified in a small way, by playing tricks upon the frequenters of the Wild Goose; putting gunpowder in their pipes, or squibs in their pockets, and astonishing them with an explosion, while they sat nodding round the fireplace in the bar-room; and if perchance a worthy burgher from some distant part of Pavonia lingered until dark over his potation, it was odds but young Vanderscamp would slip a brier under his horse's tail, as he mounted, and send him clattering along the road, in neck-or-nothing style, to the infinite astonishment and discomfiture of the rider.

It may be wondered at, that mine host of the Wild Goose did not turn such a graceless varlet out of doors; but Teunis Van Gieson was an easy tempered man, and having no child of his own, looked upon his nephew with almost parental indulgence. His patience and good nature were doomed to be tried by another intimate of his mansion. This was a cross-grained curmudgeon of a negro, named Pluto, who was a kind of enigma in Communipaw. Where he came from, nobody knew. He was found one morning, after a storm, cast like a sea-monster on the strand, in front of the Wild Goose, and lay there, more dead than alive. The neighbours gathered round, and speculated on this production of the deep; whether it were fish or flesh, or a compound of both, commonly yclept a merman. The kind-hearted Teunis Van Gieson, seeing that he wore the human form, took him into his house, and warmed him into life. By degrees, he showed signs of intelligence, and even uttered sounds very much like language, but which no one in Communipaw could understand. Some thought him a negro just from Guinea, who had either fallen overboard, or escaped from a slave-ship. Nothing, however, could ever draw from him any account of his origin. When questioned on the subject, he merely pointed to Gibbet Island, a small rocky islet, which lies in the open bay, just opposite Communipaw, as if that were his native place, though everybody knew it had never been inhabited.

In the process of time, he acquired something of the Dutch language, that is to say, he learnt all its vocabulary of oaths and maledictions, with just words sufficient to string them together. 'Donder en blicksem!' (thunder and lightning), was the gentlest of his ejaculations. For years he kept about the Wild Goose, more like one of those familiar spirits or household goblins we read of, than like a human being. He acknowledged allegiance to no one, but performed various domestic offices, when it suited his humour; waiting occasionally on the guests; grooming the horses; cutting wood; drawing water; and all this without being ordered. Lay any command on him, and the stubborn sea-urchin was sure to rebel. He was never so much at home, however, as when on the water, plying about in skiff or canoe, entirely alone, fishing, crabbing, or grabbing for oysters, and would bring home quantities for the larder of the Wild Goose, which he would throw down at the kitchen-door, with a growl. No wind nor weather deterred him from launching forth on his favourite element: indeed, the wilder the weather, the more he seemed to enjoy it. If a storm was brewing, he was sure to put off from shore; and would be seen far out in the bay, his light skiff dancing like a feather on the waves, when sea and sky were in a turmoil, and the stoutest ships were fain to lower their sails. Sometimes on such occasions he would be absent for days together. How he weathered the tempest, and how and where he subsisted, no one could divine, nor did any one venture to ask, for all had an almost superstitious awe of him. Some of the Communipaw oystermen declared they had more than once seen him suddenly disappear, canoe and all, as if plunged beneath waves, and after a while come up again, in quite a different part of the bay; whence they concluded that he could live under water like that notable species of wild duck, commonly called the hell-diver. All began to consider him in the light of a foul-weather bird, like the Mother Carey's Chicken, or petrel; and whenever they saw him putting far out in his skiff, in cloudy weather, made up their minds for a storm.

The only being for whom he seemed to have any liking, was Yan Yost Vanderscamp, and him he liked for his very wickedness. He in a manner took the boy under his tutelage, prompted him to all kinds of mischief, aided him in every wild harum-scarum freak, until the lad became the complete scapegrace of the village; a pest to his uncle, and to every one else. Nor were his pranks confined to the land; he soon learned to accompany old Pluto on the water. Together these worthies would cruise about the broad bay, and all the neighbouring straits and rivers; poking around in skiffs and canoes; robbing the set nets of the fishermen; landing on remote coasts, and laying waste orchards and water-melon patches; in short, carrying on a complete system of piracy, on a small scale. Piloted by Pluto, the youthful Vanderscamp soon became acquainted with all the bays, rivers, creeks, and inlets of the watery world around him; could navigate from the Hook to Spiting-Devil on the darkest night, and learned to set even the terrors of Hell-gate at defiance.

At length, negro and boy suddenly disappeared, and days and weeks elapsed, but without tidings of them. Some said they must have run away and gone to sea; others jocosely hinted, that old Pluto, being no other than his namesake in disguise, had spirited away the boy to the nether regions. All, however, agreed in one thing, that the village was well rid of them.

In the process of time, the good Teunis Van Gieson slept with his fathers, and the tavern remained shut up, waiting for a claimant, for the next heir was Yan Yost Vanderscamp, and he had not been heard of for years. At length, one day, a boat was seen pulling for shore, from a long, black, rakish-looking schooner, that lay at anchor in the bay. The boat's crew seemed worthy of the craft from which they debarked. Never had such a set of noisy, roistering, swaggering varlets landed in peaceful Communipaw. They were outlandish in garb and demeanour, and were headed by a rough, burly, bully ruffian, with fiery whiskers, a copper nose, a scar across his face, and a great Flaundrish beaver slouched on one side of his head, in whom, to their dismay, the quiet inhabitants were made to recognize their early pest, Yan Yost Vanderscamp. The rear of this hopeful gang was brought up by old Pluto, who had lost an eye, grown grizzly-headed, and looked more like a devil than ever. Vanderscamp renewed his acquaintance with the old burghers, much against their will, and in a manner not at all to their taste. He slapped them familiarly on the back, gave them an iron grip of the hand, and was hail fellow well met. According to his own account, he had been all the world over; had made money by bags full; had ships in every sea, and now meant to turn the Wild Goose into a country-seat, where he and his comrades, all rich merchants from foreign parts, might enjoy themselves in the interval of their voyages.

Sure enough, in a little while there was a complete metamorphose of the Wild Goose. From being a quiet, peaceful Dutch public house, it became a most riotous, uproarious private dwelling; a complete rendezvous for boisterous men of the seas, who came here to have what they called a 'blow out' on dry land, and might be seen at all hours, lounging about the door, or lolling out of the windows; swearing among themselves, and cracking rough jokes on every passer-by. The house was fitted up, too, in so strange a manner: hammocks slung to the walls, instead of bedsteads; odd kinds of furniture, of foreign fashion; bamboo couches, Spanish chairs; pistols, cutlasses, and blunderbusses, suspended on every peg; silver crucifixes on the mantel-pieces, silver candlesticks and porringers on the tables, contrasting oddly with the pewter and Delf ware of the original establishment. And then the strange amusements of these sea-monsters! Pitching Spanish dollars, instead of quoits; firing blunderbusses out of the window; shooting at a mark, or at any unhappy dog, or cat, or pig, or barn-door fowl, that might happen to come within reach.

The only being who seemed to relish their rough waggery was old Pluto; and yet he led but a dog's life of it; for they practised all kinds of manual jokes upon him; kicked him about like a football; shook him by his grizzly mop of wool, and never spoke to him without coupling a curse by way of adjective to his name, and consigning him to the infernal regions. The old fellow, however, seemed to like them better, the more they cursed him, though his utmost expression of pleasure never amounted to more than the growl of a petted bear, when his ears are rubbed.

Old Pluto was the ministering spirit at the orgies of the Wild Goose; and such orgies as took place there! Such drinking, singing, whooping, swearing; with an occasional interlude of quarrelling and fighting. The noisier grew the revel, the more old Pluto plied the potations, until the guests would become frantic in their merriment, smashing everything to pieces, and throwing the house out of the windows. Sometimes, after a drinking bout, they sallied forth and scoured the village, to the dismay of the worthy burghers, who gathered their women within doors, and would have shut up the house. Vanderscamp, however, was not to be rebuffed. He insisted on renewing acquaintance with his old neighbours, and on introducing his friends, the merchants, to their families; swore he was on the look-out for a wife, and meant, before he stopped, to find husbands for all their daughters. So, will-ye, nill-ye, sociable he was; swaggered about their best parlours, with his hat on one side of his head; sat on the good wife's nicely-waxed mahogany table, kicking his heels against the carved and polished legs; kissed and tousled the young vrouws; and if they frowned and pouted, gave them a gold rosary, or a sparkling cross, to put them in good humour again.

Sometimes nothing would satisfy him, but he must have some

of his old neighbours to dinner at the Wild Goose. There was no refusing him, for he had the complete upper hand of the community, and the peaceful burghers all stood in awe of him. But what a time would the quiet, worthy men have, among these rakehells, who would delight to astound them with the most extravagant gunpowder tales, embroidered with all kinds of foreign oaths; clink the can with them; pledge them in deep potations; bawl drinking songs in their ears, and occasionally fire pistols over their heads, or under the table, and then laugh in their faces, and ask them how they liked the smell of gunpowder.

Thus was the little village of Communipaw for a time like the unfortunate wight possessed with devils; until Vanderscamp and his brother merchants would sail on another trading voyage, when the Wild Goose would be shut up, and everything relapse into a quiet, only to be disturbed by his next visitation.

The mystery of all these proceedings gradually dawned upon the tardy intellects of Communipaw. These were the times of the notorious Captain Kidd, when the American harbours were the resorts of piratical adventurers of all kinds, who, under pretext of mercantile voyages, scoured the West Indies, made plundering descents upon the Spanish Main, visited even the remote Indian Seas, and then came to dispose of their booty, have their revels, and fit out new expeditions, in the English colonies.

Vanderscamp had served in this hopeful school, and, having risen to importance among the buccaneers, had pitched upon his native village, and early home, as a quiet, out-of-the-way, unsuspected place, where he and his comrades, while anchored at New York, might have their feasts, and concert their plans, without molestation.

At length the attention of the British government was called to these piratical enterprises, that were becoming so frequent and outrageous. Vigorous measures were taken to check and punish them. Several of the most noted freebooters were caught and executed, and three of Vanderscamp's chosen comrades, the most riotous swashbucklers of the Wild Goose, were hanged in chains on Gibbet Island, in full sight of their favourite resort. As to Vanderscamp himself, he and his man Pluto again disappeared, and it was hoped by the people of Communipaw that he had fallen in some foreign brawl, or been swung on some foreign gallows.

For a time, therefore, the tranquillity of the village was restored; the worthy Dutchmen once more smoked their pipes in peace, eyeing, with peculiar complacency, their old pests and terrors, the pirates, dangling and drying in the sun, on Gibbet Island.

This perfect calm was doomed at length to be ruffled. The fiery persecution of the pirates gradually subsided. Justice was satisfied with the examples that had been made, and there was no more talk of Kidd, and the other heroes of like kidney. On a calm summer evening, a boat, somewhat heavily laden, was seen pulling into Communipaw. What was the surprise and disquiet of the inhabitants, to see Yan Yost Vanderscamp seated at the helm, and his man Pluto tugging at the oar! Vanderscamp, however, was apparently an altered man. He brought home with him a wife, who seemed to be a shrew, and to have the upper hand of him. He no longer was the swaggering, bully ruffian, but affected the regular merchant, and talked of retiring from business, and settling down quietly, to pass the rest of his days in his native place.

The Wild Goose mansion was again opened, but with diminished splendour, and no riot. It is true, Vanderscamp had frequently nautical visitors, and the sound of revelry was occasionally overheard in his house; but everything seemed to be done under the rose; and old Pluto was the only servant that officiated at these orgies. The visitors, indeed, were by no means of the turbulent stamp of their predecessors; but quiet, mysterious traders, full of nods, and winks, and hieroglyphic signs, with whom, to use their cant phrase, 'everything was snug'. Their ships came to anchor at night, in the lower bay; and, on a private signal, Vanderscamp would launch his boat, and accompanied solely by his man Pluto, would make them mysterious visits. Sometimes boats pulled in at night, in front of the Wild Goose, and various articles of merchandise were landed in the dark, and spirited away, nobody knew whither.

One of the more curious of the inhabitants kept watch, and caught a glimpse of the features of some of these night visitors, by the casual glance of a lantern, and declared that he recognised more than one of the freebooting frequenters of the Wild Goose, in former times; whence he concluded that Vanderscamp was at his old game, and that this mysterious merchandise was nothing more nor less than piratical plunder. The more charitable opinion, however, was, that Vanderscamp and his comrades, having been driven from their old line of business by the 'oppressions of government', had resorted to smuggling to make both ends meet.

Be that as it may: I come now to the extraordinary fact, which is the butt-end of this story. It happened late one night, that Yan Yost Vanderscamp was returning across the broad bay, in his light skiff, rowed by his man Pluto. He had been carousing on board of a vessel newly arrived, and was somewhat obfuscated in intellect by the liquor he had imbibed. It was a still, sultry night; a heavy mass of lurid clouds was rising in the west, with the low muttering of distant thunder. Vanderscamp called on Pluto to pull lustily, that they might get home before the gathering storm. The old negro made no reply, but shaped his course so as to skirt the rocky shores of Gibbet Island. A faint creaking overhead caused Vanderscamp to cast up his eyes, when to his horror he beheld the bodies of three pot companions and brothers in iniquity dangling in the moonlight, their rags fluttering, and their chains creaking, as they were slowly swung backward and forward by the rising breeze.

'What do you mean, you blockhead!' cried Vanderscamp, 'by pulling so close to the island?'

'I thought you'd be glad to see your old friends once more,' growled the negro: 'you were never afraid of a living man, what do you fear from the dead?'

'Who's afraid?' hiccupped Vanderscamp, partly heated by liquor, partly nettled by the jeer of the negro; 'who's afraid! Hang me, but I would be glad to see them once more, alive or dead, at the Wild Goose. Come, my lads in the wind!' continued he, taking a draught, and flourishing the bottle above his head, 'here's fair weather to you in the other world; and if you should be walking the rounds tonight, odds fish! but I'll be happy if you will drop in to supper.'

A dismal creaking was the only reply. The wind blew loud and shrill, and as it whistled round the gallows, and among the bones, sounded as if they were laughing and gibbering in the air. Old Pluto chuckled to himself, and now pulled home. The storm burst over the voyagers, while they were yet far from shore. The rain fell in torrents, the thunder crashed and pealed, and the lightning kept up an incessant blaze. It was stark midnight before they landed at Communipaw.

Dripping and shivering, Vanderscamp crawled homeward. He was completely sobered by the storm; the water soaked from without having diluted and cooled the liquor within. Arrived at the Wild Goose, he knocked timidly and dubiously at the door, for he dreaded the reception he was to receive from his wife. He had reason to do so. She met him at the threshold, in a precious ill-humour.

'Is this a time,' said she, 'to keep people out of their beds, and to bring home company, to turn the house upside down?'

'Company?' said Vanderscamp, meekly; 'I have brought no company with me, wife.'

'No, indeed! they have got here before you, but by your invitation; and blessed-looking company they are, truly!'

Vanderscamp's knees smote together. 'For the love of heaven, where are they, wife?'

'Where?—why in the blue-room, upstairs; making themselves as much at home as if the house were their own.'

Vanderscamp made a desperate effort, scrambled up to the room, and threw open the door. Sure enough, there, at a table. on which burned a light as blue as brimstone, sat the three guests from Gibbet Island, with halters round their necks, and bobbing their cups together, as they were hob-a-nobbing, and trolling the old Dutch freebooters' glee, since translated into English:-

> *For three merry lads be we,*
> *And three merry lads be we:*

I on the land, and thou on the sand,
And Jack on the gallows-tree.

Vanderscamp saw and heard no more. Starting back with horror, he missed his footing on the landing-place, and fell from the top of the stairs to the bottom. He was taken up speechless, and, either from the fall or the fright, was buried in the yard of the little Dutch church at Bergen, on the following Sunday.

From that day forward, the fate of the Wild Goose was sealed. It was pronounced a *haunted house*, and avoided accordingly. No one inhabited it but Vanderscamp's shrew of a widow, and old Pluto, and they were considered but little better than its hobgoblin visitors. Pluto grew more and more haggard and morose, and looked more like an imp of darkness than a human being. He spoke to no one, but went about muttering to himself, or, as some hinted, talking with the devil, who, though unseen, was ever at his elbow. Now and then he was seen pulling about the bay alone in his skiff in dark weather, or at the approach of nightfall; nobody could tell why, unless on an errand to invite more guests from the gallows. Indeed it was affirmed that the Wild Goose still continued to be a house of entertainment for such guests, and that on stormy nights, the blue chamber was occasionally illuminated, and sounds of diabolical merriment were overheard, mingling with the howling of the tempest. Some treated these as idle stories, until on one such night, it was about the time of the equinox, there was a horrible uproar in the Wild Goose, that could not be mistaken. It was not so much the sound of revelry, however, as strife, with two or three piercing shrieks, that pervaded every part of the village. Nevertheless, no one thought of hastening to the spot. On the contrary, the honest burghers of Communipaw drew their nightcaps over their ears, and buried their heads under the bedclothes, at the thoughts of Vanderscamp and his gallows companions.

The next morning, some of the bolder and more curious undertook to reconnoitre. All was quiet and lifeless at the Wild Goose. The door yawned wide open, and had evidently been open all night, for the storm had beaten into the house.

Gathering more courage from the silence and apparent desertion, they gradually ventured over the threshold. The house had indeed the air of having been possessed by devils. Everything was topsy-turvy; trunks had been broken open, and chests of drawers and corner cupboards turned inside out, as in a time of general sack and pillage; but the most woeful sight was the widow of Yan Yost Vanderscamp, extended a corpse on the floor of the blue chamber, with the marks of a deadly gripe on the windpipe.

All now was conjecture and dismay at Communipaw; and the disappearance of old Pluto, who was nowhere to be found, gave rise to all kinds of wild surmises. Some suggested that the negro had betrayed the house to some of Vanderscamp's buccaneering associates, and that they had decamped together with the booty; other surmised that the negro was nothing more nor less than a devil incarnate, who had now accomplished his ends, and made off with his dues.

Events, however, vindicated the negro from this last imputation. His skiff was picked up, drifting about the bay, bottom upward, as if wrecked in a tempest; and his body was found, shortly afterwards, by some Communipaw fishermen, stranded among the rocks of Gibbet Island, near the foot of the pirates' gallows. The fishermen shook their heads, and observed that old Pluto had ventured once too often to invite guests from Gibbet Island.

from *Wolfert's Roost*

LEGEND OF THE ARABIAN ASTROLOGER

In old times, many hundred years ago, there was a Moorish king named Aben Habuz, who reigned over the kingdom of Granada. He was a retired conqueror, that is to say, one who having in his more youthful days led a life of constant foray and depredation, now that he was grown feeble and superannuated, 'languished for repose', and desired nothing more than to live at peace with all the world, to husband his laurels, and to enjoy in quiet the possessions he had wrested from his neighbours.

It so happened, however, that this most reasonable and pacific old monarch had young rivals to deal with; princes full of his early passion for fame and fighting, and who were disposed to call him to account for the scores he had run up with their fathers. Certain distant districts of his own territories, also, which during the days of his vigour he had treated with a high hand, were prone, now that he languished for repose, to rise in rebellion and threaten to invest him in his capital. Thus he had foes on every side; and as Granada is surrounded by wild and craggy mountains, which hide the approach of an enemy, the unfortunate Aben Habuz was kept in a constant state of vigilance and alarm, not knowing in what quarter hostilities might break out.

It was in vain that he built watchtowers on the mountains, and stationed guards at every pass with orders to make fires by night and smoke by day, on the approach of an enemy. His alert foes, baffling every precaution, would break out of some unthought-of defile, ravage his lands beneath his very nose, and then make off with prisoners and booty to the mountains. Was ever peaceable and retired conqueror in a more uncomfortable predicament?

While Aben Habuz was harassed by these perplexities and molestations, an ancient Arabian physician arrived at his court. His grey beard descended to his girdle, and he had every mark of extreme age, yet he had travelled almost the whole way from Egypt on foot, with no other aid than a staff, marked with hieroglyphics. His fame had preceded him. His name was Ibrahim Ebn Abu Ayub, he was said to have lived ever since the days of Mahomet, and to be the son of Abu Ayub, the last of the companions of the Prophet. He had, when a child, followed the conquering army of Amru into Egypt, where he had remained many years studying the dark sciences, and particularly magic, among the Egyptian priests.

It was, moreover, said that he had found out the secret of prolonging life, by means of which he had arrived to the great age of upwards of two centuries, though, as he did not discover the secret until well stricken in years, he could only perpetuate his grey hair and wrinkles.

This wonderful old man was honorably entertained by the king; who, like most superannuated monarchs, began to take physicians into great favour. He would have assigned him an apartment in his palace, but the astrologer preferred a cave in the side of the hill which rises above the city of Granada, being the same on which the Alhambra has since been built. He caused the cave to be enlarged so as to form a spacious and lofty hall, with a circular hole at the top, through which, as through a well, he could see the heavens and behold the stars even at mid-day. The walls of this hall were covered with Egyptian hieroglyphics, with cabbalistic symbols, and with the figures of the stars in their signs. This hall he furnished with many implements, fabricated under his directions by cunning artificers of Granada, but the occult properties of which were known only to himself.

In a little while the sage Ibrahim became the bosom

counsellor of the king, who applied to him for advice in every emergency. Aben Habuz was once inveighing against the injustice of his neighbours, and bewailing the restless vigilance he had to observe to guard himself against their invasions; when he had finished, the astrologer remained silent for a moment, and then replied: 'Know, O King, that when I was in Egypt I beheld a great marvel devised by a pagan priestess of old. On a mountain, above the city of Borsa, and overlooking the great valley of the Nile, was a figure of a ram, and above it a figure of a cock, both of molten brass, and turning upon a pivot. Whenever the country was threatened with invasion, the ram would turn in the direction of the enemy, and the cock would crow; upon this the inhabitants of the city knew of the danger, and of the quarter from which it was approaching, and could take timely means to guard against it.'

'God is great!' exclaimed the pacific Aben Habuz, 'what a treasure would be such a ram to keep an eye upon these mountains around me; and then such a cock, to crow in time of danger! Allah Akbar! how securely I might sleep in my palace with such sentinels on the top!'

The astrologer waited until the ecstasies of the king had subsided, and then proceeded.

'After the victorious Amru (may he rest in peace!) had finished his conquest of Egypt, I remained among the priests of the land, studying the rites and ceremonies of their idolatrous faith, and seeking to make myself master of the hidden knowledge for which they are renowned. I was one day seated on the banks of the Nile, conversing with an ancient priest, when he pointed to the mighty pyramids which rose like mountains out of the neighbouring desert. "All that we can teach thee," said he, "is nothing to the knowledge locked up in those mighty piles. In the centre of the central pyramid is a sepulchral chamber, in which is inclosed the mummy of the high-priest, who aided in rearing that stupendous pile; and with him is buried a wondrous book of knowledge containing all the secrets of magic and art. This book was given to Adam after his fall, and was handed down from generation to generation to King Solomon the wise, and by its aid he built the temple of Jerusalem. How it came into the possession of the builder of the pyramids, is known to him alone who knows all things."

'When I heard these words of the Egyptian priest, my heart burned to get possession of that book. I could command the services of many of the soldiers of our conquering army, and of a number of the native Egyptians: with these I set to work, and pierced the solid mass of the pyramid, until, after great toil, I came upon one of its interior and hidden passages. Following this up, and threading a fearful labyrinth, I penetrated into the very heart of the pyramid, even to the sepulchral chamber, where the mummy of the high-priest had lain for ages. I broke through the outer cases of the mummy, unfolded its many wrappers and bandages, and at length found the precious volume on its bosom. I seized it with a trembling hand, and groped my way out of the pyramid, leaving the mummy in its dark and silent sepulchre, there to await the final day of resurrection and judgment.'

'Son of Abu Ayub,' exclaimed Aben Habuz, 'thou hast been a great traveller, and seen marvellous things; but of what avail to me is the secret of the pyramid, and the volume of knowledge of the wise Solomon?'

'This it is, O king! By the study of that book I am instructed in all magic arts, and can command the assistance of genii to accomplish my plans. The mystery of the Talisman of Borsa is therefore familiar to me, and such a talisman can I make; nay, one of greater virtues.'

'O wise son of Abu Ayub,' cried Aben Habuz, 'better were such a talisman, than all the watchtowers on the hills, and sentinels upon the borders. Give me such a safeguard, and the riches of my treasury are at thy command.'

The astrologer immediately set to work to gratify the wishes of the monarch. He caused a great tower to be erected upon the top of the royal palace, which stood on the brow of the hill of the Albaycin. The tower was built of stones brought from Egypt, and taken, it is said, from one of the pyramids. In the upper part of the tower was a circular hall, with windows looking towards every point of the compass, and before each window was a table, on which was arranged, as on a chessboard, a mimic army of horse and foot, with the effigy of the potentate that ruled in that direction, all carved of wood. To each of these tables there was a small lance, no bigger than a bodkin, on which were engraved certain Chaldaic characters. This hall was kept constantly closed, by a gate of brass, with a great lock of steel, the key of which was in possession of the king.

On the top of the tower was a bronze figure of a Moorish horseman, fixed on a pivot, with a shield on one arm, and his lance elevated perpendicularly. The face of this horseman was towards the city, as if keeping guard over it; but if any foe were at hand, the figure would turn in that direction, and would level the lance as if for action.

When this talisman was finished, Aben Habuz was all impatient to try its virtues; and longed as ardently for an invasion as he had ever sighed after repose. His desire was soon gratified. Tidings were brought, early one morning, by the sentinel appointed to watch the tower, that the face of the bronze horseman was turned towards the mountains of Elvira, and that his lance pointed directly against the Pass of Lope.

'Let the drums and trumpets sound to arms, and all Granada be put on the alert,' said Aben Habuz.

'O king,' said the astrologer, 'let not your city be disquieted nor your warriors called to arms; we need no aid of force to deliver you from your enemies. Dismiss your attendants, and let us proceed alone to the secret hall of the tower.'

The ancient Aben Habuz mounted the staircase of the tower, leaning on the arm of the still more ancient Ibrahim Ebn Abu Ayub. They unlocked the brazen door and entered. The window that looked towards the Pass of Lope was open. 'In this direction,' said the astrologer, 'lies the danger; approach, O king, and behold the mystery of the table.'

King Aben Habuz approached the seeming chessboard, on which were arranged the small wooden effigies, when, to his surprise, he perceived that they were all in motion. The horses pranced and curveted, the warriors brandished their weapons, and there was a faint sound of drums and trumpets, and the clang of arms, and neighing of steeds; but all no louder, nor more distinct, than the hum of the bee, or the summer-fly, in the drowsy ear of him who lies at noontide in the shade.

'Behold, O king,' said the astrologer, 'a proof that thy enemies are even now in the field. They must be advancing through yonder mountains, by the Pass of Lope. Would you produce a panic and confusion amongst them, and cause them to retreat without loss of life, strike these effigies with the butt-end of this magic lance; would you cause bloody feud and carnage, strike with the point.'

A livid streak passed across the countenance of Aben Habuz; he seized the lance with trembling eagerness; his grey beard wagged with exultation as he tottered toward the table: 'Son of Abu Ayub,' exclaimed he, in chuckling tone, 'I think we will have a little blood!'

So saying, he thrust the magic lance into some of the pigmy effigies, and belaboured others with the butt-end, upon which the former fell as dead upon the board, and the rest turning upon each other began, pell-mell, a chance-medley fight.

It was with difficulty the astrologer could stay the hand of the most pacific of monarchs, and prevent him from absolutely exterminating his foes; at length he prevailed upon him to leave the tower, and to send out scouts to the mountains by the Pass of Lope.

They returned with the intelligence, that a Christian army had advanced through the heart of the Sierra, almost within sight of Granada, where a dissension had broken out among them; they had turned their weapons against each other, and after much slaughter had retreated over the border.

Aben Habuz was transported with joy on thus proving the efficacy of the talisman. 'At length,' said he, 'I shall lead a life of tranquillity, and have all my enemies in my power. O wise son of Abu Ayub, what can I bestow on thee in reward for such a blessing?'

'The wants of an old man and a philosopher, O king, are few and simple; grant me but the means of fitting up my cave as a suitable hermitage, and I am content.'

'How noble is the moderation of the truly wise!' exclaimed Abu Habuz, secretly pleased at the cheapness of the recompense. He summoned his treasurer, and bade him dispense whatever sums might be required by Ibrahim to complete and furnish his hermitage.

The astrologer now gave orders to have various chambers hewn out of the solid rock, so as to form ranges of apartments connected with his astrological hall; these he caused to be furnished with luxurious ottomans and divans, and the walls to be hung with the richest silks of Damascus. 'I am an old man,' said he, 'and can no longer rest my bones on stone couches, and these damp walls require covering.'

He had baths too constructed, and provided with all kinds of perfumes and aromatic oils: 'For a bath,' said he, 'is necessary to counteract the rigidity of age, and to restore freshness and suppleness to the frame withered by study.'

He caused the apartments to be hung with innumerable silver and crystal lamps, which he filled with a fragrant oil, prepared according to a receipt discovered by him in the tombs of Egypt. This oil was perpetual in its nature, and diffused a soft radiance like the tempered light of day. 'The light of the sun,' said he, 'is too garish and violent for the eyes of an old man, and the light of the lamp is more congenial to the studies of a philosopher.'

The treasurer of king Aben Habuz groaned at the sums daily demanded to fit up this hermitage, and he carried his complaints to the king. The royal word, however, had been given; Aben Habuz shrugged his shoulders: 'We must have patience,' said he, 'this old man has taken his idea of a philosophic retreat from the interior of the pyramids, and of the vast ruins of Egypt; but all things have an end, and so will the furnishing of his cavern.'

The king was in the right; the hermitage was at length complete, and formed a sumptuous subterranean palace. The astrologer expressed himself perfectly content, and, shutting himself up, remained for three whole days buried in study. At the end of that time he appeared again before the treasurer.

'One thing more is necessary,' said he, 'one trifling solace for the intervals of mental labour.'

'O wise Ibrahim, I am bound to furnish everything necessary for thy solitude; what more dost thou require?'

'I would fain have a few dancing women.'

'Dancing women!' echoed the treasurer, with surprise.

'Dancing women,' replied the sage, gravely; 'and let them be young and fair to look upon; for the sight of youth and beauty is refreshing. A few will suffice, for I am a philosopher of simple habits and easily satisfied.'

While the philosophic Ibrahim Ebn Abu Ayub passed his time thus sagely in his hermitage, the pacific Aben Habuz carried on furious campaigns in effigy in his tower. It was a glorious thing for an old man, like himself, of quiet habits, to have war made easy, and to be enabled to amuse himself in his chamber by brushing away whole armies like so many swarms of flies.

For a time he rioted in the indulgence of his humours, and even taunted and insulted his neighbours, to induce them to make incursions; but by degrees they grew wary from repeated disasters until no one ventured to invade his territories. For many months the bronze horseman remained on the peace establishment with his lance elevated in the air, and the worthy old monarch began to repine at the want of his accustomed sport, and to grow peevish at his monotonous tranquillity.

At length, one day, the talismanic horseman veered suddenly round, and lowering his lance, made a dead point towards the mountains of Guadix. Aben Habuz hastened to his tower, but the magic table in that direction remained quiet; not a single warrior was in motion. Perplexed at the circumstance, he sent forth a troop of horse to scour the mountains and reconnoitre. They returned after three days' absence.

'We have searched every mountain pass,' said they, 'but not a helm nor spear was stirring. All that we have found in the course of our foray, was a Christian damsel of surpassing beauty, sleeping at noontide beside a fountain, whom we have brought away captive.'

'A damsel of surpassing beauty!' exclaimed Aben Habuz, his eyes gleaming with animation; 'let her be conducted into my presence.'

The beautiful damsel was accordingly conducted into his presence. She was arrayed with all the luxury of ornament that had prevailed among the Gothic Spaniards at the time of the Arabian conquest. Pearls of dazzling whiteness were entwined with her raven tresses; and jewels sparkled on her forehead, rivalling the lustre of her eyes. Around her neck was a golden chain, to which was suspended a silver lyre, which hung by her side.

The flashes of her dark refulgent eye were like sparks of fire on the withered, yet combustible, heart of Aben Habuz; the swimming voluptuousness of her gait made his senses reel. 'Fairest of women,' cried he, with rapture, 'who and what art thou?'

'The daughter of one of the Gothic princes, who but lately ruled over this land. The armies of my father have been destroyed, as if by magic, among these mountains; he has been driven into exile, and his daughter is a captive.'

'Beware, O king!' whispered Ibrahim Ebn Abu Ayub, 'this may be one of these northern sorceresses of whom we have heard, who assume the most seductive forms to beguile the unwary. Methinks I read witchcraft in her eye, and sorcery in every movement. Doubtless this is the enemy pointed out by the talisman.'

'Son of Abu Ayub,' replied the king, 'thou art a wise man, I grant, a conjuror for aught I know; but thou art little versed in the ways of woman. In that knowledge will I yield to no man; no, not to the wise Solomon himself, notwithstanding the number of his wives and concubines. As to this damsel, I see no harm in her; she is fair to look upon, and finds favour in my eyes.'

'Hearken, O king,' replied the astrologer. 'I have given thee many victories by means of my talisman, but have never shared any of the spoil. Give me then this stray captive, to solace me in my solitude with her silver lyre. If she be indeed a sorceress, I have counter spells that set her charms at defiance.'

'What! more women!' cried Aben Habuz. 'Hast thou not already dancing women enough to solace thee?'

'Dancing women have I, it is true, but no singing women. I would fain have a little minstrelsy to refresh my mind when weary with the toils of study.'

'A truce with thy hermit cravings,' said the king, impatiently. 'This damsel have I marked for my own. I see much comfort in her; even such comfort as David, the father of Solomon the wise, found in the society of Abishag the Shunamite.'

Further solicitations and remonstrances of the astrologer only provoked a more peremptory reply from the monarch, and they parted in high displeasure. The sage shut himself up in his hermitage to brood over his disappointment; ere he departed, however, he gave the king one more warning to beware of his dangerous captive. But where is the old man in love that will listen to council? Aben Habuz resigned himself to the full sway of his passion. His only study was how to render himself amiable in the eyes of the Gothic beauty. He had not youth to recommend him, it is true, but then he had riches; and when a lover is old, he is generally generous. The Zacatin of Granada was ransacked for the most precious merchandise of the East; silks, jewels, precious gems, exquisite perfumes, all that Asia and Africa yielded of rich and rare, were lavished upon the princess. All kinds of spectacles and festivities were devised for her entertainment; minstrelsy, dancing, tournaments, bull-fights:— Granada for a time was a scene of perpetual pageant. The Gothic princess regarded all this splendour with the air of one accustomed to magnificence. She received everything as a homage due to her rank, or rather to her beauty; for beauty is more lofty in its exactions even than rank. Nay, she seemed to take a secret pleasure in exciting the monarch to expenses that made his treasury shrink; and then treating his extravagant generosity as a mere matter of course. With all his assiduity and munificence, also, the venerable lover could not flatter himself that he had made any impression on her heart. She never frowned on him, it is true, but then she never smiled. Whenever he began to plead his passion, she struck her silver lyre. There was a mystic charm in the sound. In an instant the monarch began to nod; a drowsiness stole over him, and he gradually sank into a sleep, from which he awoke wonderfully refreshed, but perfectly cooled for the time of his passion. This was very baffling to his suit; but then these slumbers were accompanied by agreeable dreams, which completely inthralled the senses of the drowsy lover; so he continued to dream on, while all Granada scoffed at his infatuation, and groaned at the treasures lavished for a song.

At length a danger burst on the head of Aben Habuz, against which his talisman yielded him no warning. An insurrection broke out in his very capital; his palace was surrounded by an armed rabble, who menaced his life and the life of his Christian paramour. A spark of his ancient warlike spirit was awakened in the breast of the monarch. At the head of a handful of his guards he sallied forth, put the rebels to flight, and crushed the insurrection in the bud.

When quiet was again restored, he sought the astrologer, who still remained shut up in his hermitage, chewing the bitter cud of resentment.

Aben Habuz approached him with a conciliatory tone, 'O wise son of Abu Ayub,' said he, 'well didst thou predict dangers to me from this captive beauty: tell me then, thou who art so quick at foreseeing peril, what I should do to avert it.'

'Put from thee the infidel damsel who is the cause.'

'Sooner would I part with my kingdom,' cried Aben Habuz.

'Thou art in danger of losing both,' replied the astrologer.

'Be not harsh and angry, O most profound of philosophers; consider the double distress of a monarch and a lover, and devise some means of protecting me from the evils by which I am menaced. I care not for grandeur, I care not for power, I languish only for repose; would that I had some quiet retreat where I might take refuge from the world, and all its cares, and pomps, and troubles, and devote the remainders of my days to tranquillity and love.'

The astrologer regarded him for a moment, from under his bushy eyebrows.

'And what wouldst thou give, if I could provide thee such a retreat?'

'Thou shouldst name thy own reward, and whatever it might be, if within the scope of my power, as my soul liveth, it should be thine.'

'Thou hast heard, O king, of the garden of Irem, one of the prodigies of Arabia the happy.'

'I have heard of that garden; it is recorded in the Koran, even in the chapter entitled "The Dawn of Day". I have moreover, heard marvellous things related of it by pilgrims who had been to Mecca; but I considered them wild fables, such as travellers are wont to tell who have visited remote countries.'

'Discredit not, O king, the tales of travellers,' rejoined the astrologer, gravely, 'for they contain precious rarities of knowledge brought from the ends of the earth. As to the palace and garden of Irem, what is generally told of them is true; I have seen them with mine own eyes—listen to my adventure; for it has a bearing upon the object of your request.

'In my younger days, when a mere Arab of the desert, I tended my father's camels. In traversing the desert of Aden, one of them strayed from the rest, and was lost. I searched after it for several days, but in vain, until, wearied and faint, I laid myself down at noontide, and slept under a palm-tree by the side of a scanty well. When I awoke, I found myself at the gate of a city. I entered, and beheld noble streets, and squares, and market-places; but all were silent and without an inhabitant. I wandered on until I came to a sumptuous palace with a garden adorned with fountains and fishponds, and groves and flowers, and orchards laden with delicious fruit; but still no one was to be seen. Upon which, appalled at this loneliness, I hastened to depart; and, after issuing forth at the gate of the city, I turned to look upon the place, but it was no longer to be seen; nothing but the silent desert extended before my eyes.

'In the neighbourhood I met with an aged dervish, learned in the traditions and secrets of the land, and related to him what had befallen me. "This," said he, "is the far-famed garden of Irem, one of the wonders of the desert. It only appears at times to some wanderer like thyself, gladdening him with the sight of towers and palaces and garden walls overhung with richly-laden fruit-trees, and then vanishes, leaving nothing but a lonely desert. And this is the story of it. In old times, when this country was inhabited by the Addites, King Sheddad, the son of Ad, the great grandson of Noah, founded here a splendid city. When it was finished, and he saw its grandeur, his heart was puffed up with pride and arrogance, and he determined to build a royal palace, with gardens which should rival all related in the Koran of the celestial paradise. But the curse of heaven fell upon him for his presumption. He and his subjects were swept from the earth, and his splendid city, and palace, and gardens, were laid under a perpetual spell, which hides them from human sight, excepting that they are seen at intervals, by way of keeping his sin in perpetual remembrance."

'This story, O king, and the wonders I had seen, ever dwelt in my mind; and in after years, when I had been in Egypt, and was possessed of the book of knowledge of Solomon the wise, I determined to return and revisit the garden of Irem. I did so, and found it revealed to my instructed sight. I took possession of the palace of Sheddad, and passed several days in his mock paradise. The genii who watch over the place, were obedient to my magic power, and revealed to me the spells by which the whole garden had been, as it were, conjured into existence, and by which it was rendered invisible. Such a palace and garden, O king, can I make for thee, even here, on the mountain above the city. Do I not know all the secret spells? and am I not in possession of the book of knowledge of Solomon the wise?'

'O wise son of Abu Ayub!' exclaimed Aben Habuz, trembling with eagerness, 'thou art a traveller indeed, and hast seen and learned marvellous things! Contrive me such a paradise, and ask any reward, even to the half of my kingdom.'

'Alas!' replied the other, 'thou knowest I am an old man, and a philosopher, and easily satisfied; all the reward I ask is the first beast of burden, with its load, which shall enter the magic portal of the palace.'

The monarch gladly agreed to so moderate a stipulation, and

the astrologer began his work. On the summit of the hill, immediately above his subterranean hermitage, he caused a great gateway or barbican to be erected, opening through the centre of a strong tower.

There was an outer vestibule or porch, with a lofty arch, and within it a portal secured by massive gates. On the key-stone of the portal the astrologer, with his own hand, wrought the figure of a huge key; and on the key-stone of the outer arch of the vestibule, which was loftier than that of the portal, he carved a gigantic hand. These were potent talismans, over which he repeated many sentences in an unknown tongue.

When this gateway was finished he shut himself up for two days in his astrological hall, engaged in secret incantations; on the third he ascended the hill, and passed the whole day on its summit. At a late hour of the night he came down, and presented himself before Aben Habuz. 'At length, O king,' said he, 'my labour is accomplished. On the summit of the hill stands one of the most delectable palaces that ever the head of man devised, or the heart of man desired. It contains sumptuous halls and galleries, delicious gardens, cool fountains, and fragrant baths; in a word, the whole mountain is converted into a paradise. Like the garden of Irem, it is protected by a mighty charm, which hides it from the view and search of mortals, excepting such as possess the secret of its talismans.'

'Enough!' cried Aben Habuz, joyfully, 'tomorrow morning with the first light we will ascend and take possession.' The happy monarch slept but little that night. Scarcely had the rays of the sun begun to play about the snowy summit of the Sierra Nevada, when he mounted his steed, and, accompanied only by a few chosen attendants, ascended a steep and narrow road leading up the hill. Beside him, on a white palfrey, rode the Gothic princess, her whole dress sparkling with jewels, while round her neck was suspended her silver lyre. The astrologer walked on the other side of the king, assisting his steps with his hieroglyphic staff, for he never mounted steed of any kind.

Aben Habuz looked to see the towers of the palace brightening above him, and the imbowered terraces of its gardens stretching along the heights; but as yet nothing of the kind was to be descried. 'That is the mystery and safeguard of the place,' said the astrologer, 'nothing can be discerned until you have passed the spell-bound gateway, and been put in possession of the palace.'

As they approached the gateway, the astrologer paused, and pointed out to the king the mystic hand and key carved upon the portal of the arch. 'These,' said he, 'are the talismans which guard the entrance to this paradise. Until yonder hand shall reach down and seize that key, neither mortal power nor magic artifice can prevail against the lord of this mountain.'

While Aben Habuz was gazing, with open mouth and silent wonder, at these mystic talismans, the palfrey of the princess proceeded, and bore her in at the portal, to the very centre of the barbican.

'Behold,' cried the astrologer, 'my promised reward; the first animal with its burden which should enter the magic gateway.'

Aben Habuz smiled at what he considered a pleasantry of the ancient man; but when he found him to be in earnest, his grey beard trembled with indignation.

'Son of Abu Ayub,' said he, sternly, 'what equivocation is this? Thou knowest the meaning of my promise: the first beast of burden, with its load, that should enter this portal. Take the strongest mule in my stables, load it with the most precious things of my treasury, and it is thine; but dare not raise thy thoughts to her who is the delight of my heart.'

'What need I of wealth,' cried the astrologer, scornfully; 'have I not the book of knowledge of Solomon the wise, and through it the command of the secret treasures of the earth? The princess is mine by right; thy royal word is pledged: I claim her as my own.'

The princess looked down haughtily from her palfrey, and a light smile of scorn curled her rosy lip at this dispute between two grey-beards, for the possession of youth and beauty. The wrath of the monarch got the better of his discretion. 'Base son of the desert,' cried he, 'thou may'st be master of many arts, but know me for thy master, and presume not to juggle with thy king.'

'My master! my king!' echoed the astrologer—'The monarch of a mole-hill to claim sway over him who possesses the talismans of Solomon! Farewell, Aben Habuz; reign over thy petty kingdom, and revel in thy paradise of fools; for me, I will laugh at thee in my philosophic retirement.'

So saying he seized the bridle of the palfrey, smote the earth with his staff, and sank with the Gothic princess through the centre of the barbican. The earth closed over them, and no trace remained of the opening by which they had descended.

Aben Habuz was struck dumb for a time with astonishment. Recovering himself, he ordered a thousand workmen to dig, with pickaxe and spade, into the ground where the astrologer had disappeared. They digged and digged, but in vain; the flinty bosom of the hill resisted their implements; or if they did penetrate a little way, the earth filled in again as fast as they threw it out. Aben Habuz sought the mouth of the cavern at the foot of the hill, leading to the subterranean palace of the astrologer; but it was nowhere to be found. Where once had been an entrance, was now a solid surface of primeval rock. With the disappearance of Ibrahim Ebn Abu Ayub ceased the benefit of his talismans. The bronze horseman remained fixed, with his face turned toward the hill, and his spear pointed to the spot where the astrologer had descended, as if there still lurked the deadliest foe of Aben Habuz.

From time to time the sound of music, and the tones of a female voice, could be faintly heard from the bosom of the hill; and a peasant one day brought word to the king, that in the preceding night he had found a fissure in the rock, by which he had crept in, until he looked down into a subterranean hall, in which sat the astrologer, on a magnificent divan, slumbering and nodding to the silver lyre of the princess, which seemed to hold a magic sway over his senses.

Aben Habuz sought the fissure in the rock, but it was again closed. He renewed the attempt to unearth his rival, but all in vain. The spell of the hand and key was too potent to be counteracted by human power. As to the summit of the mountain, the site of the promised palace and garden, it remained a naked waste; either the boasted elysium was hidden from sight by enchantment, or was a mere fable of the astrologer. The world charitably supposed the latter, and some used to call the place 'The King's Folly', while the others named it 'The Fool's Paradise'.

To add to the chagrin of Aben Habuz, the neighbours whom he had defied and taunted, and cut up at his leisure while master of the talismanic horseman, finding him no longer protected by magic spell, made inroads into his territories from all sides, and the remainder of the life of the most pacific of monarchs was a tissue of turmoils.

At length Aben Habuz died, and was buried. Ages have since rolled away. The Alhambra has been built on the eventful mountain, and in some measure realises the fabled delights of the garden of Irem. The spell-bound gateway still exists entire, protected no doubt by the mystic hand and key, and now forms the Gate of Justice, the grand entrance to the fortress. Under that gateway, it is said, the old astrologer remains in his subterranean hall, nodding on his divan, lulled by the silver lyre of the princess.

The old invalid sentinels who mount guard at the gate hear the strains occasionally in the summer nights; and, yielding to their soporific power, doze quietly at their posts. Nay, so drowsy an influence pervades the place, that even those who watch by day may generally be seen nodding on the stone benches of the barbican, or sleeping under the neighbouring trees; so that in fact it is the drowsiest military post in all Christendom. All this, say the ancient legends, will endure from age to age. The princess will remain captive to the astrologer; and the astrologer, bound up in magic slumber by the princess, until the last day, unless the mystic hand shall grasp the fated key, and dispel the whole charm of this enchanted mountain.

from *The Alhambra*

THE DEVIL AND TOM WALKER

A few miles from Boston in Massachusetts, there is a deep inlet, winding several miles into the interior of the country from Charles Bay, and terminating in a thickly-wooded swamp or morass. On one side of this inlet is a beautiful dark grove; on the opposite side the land rises abruptly from the water's edge into a high ridge, on which grow a few scattered oaks of great age and immense size. Under one of these gigantic trees, according to old stories, there was a great amount of treasure buried by Kidd the pirate. The inlet allowed a facility to bring the money in a boat secretly and at night to the very foot of the hill; the elevation of the place permitted a good lookout to be kept that no one was at hand; while the remarkable trees formed good landmarks by which the place might easily be found again. The old stories add, moreover, that the devil presided at the hiding of the money, and took it under his guardianship; but this it is well known he always does with buried treasure, particularly when it has been ill-gotten. Be that as it may, Kidd never returned to recover his wealth; being shortly after seized at Boston, sent out to England, and there hanged for a pirate.

About the year 1727, just at the time that earthquakes were prevalent in New England, and shook many tall sinners down upon their knees, there lived near this place a meagre, miserly fellow of the name of Tom Walker. He had a wife as miserly as himself: they were so miserly that they even conspired to cheat each other. Whatever the woman could lay hands on, she hid away; a hen could not cackle but she was on the alert to secure the new-laid egg. Her husband was continually prying about to detect her secret hoards, and many and fierce were the conflicts that took place about what ought to have been common property. They lived in a forlorn-looking house that stood alone, and had an air of starvation. A few straggling savin-trees, emblems of sterility, grew near it; no smoke ever curled from its chimney; no traveller stopped at its door. A miserable horse, whose ribs were as articulate as the bars of a gridiron, stalked about a field, where a thin carpet of moss, scarcely covering the ragged beds of puddingstone, tantalized and balked his hunger; and sometimes he would lean his head over the fence, look piteously at the passer-by, and seem to petition deliverance from this land of famine.

The house and its inmates had altogether a bad name. Tom's wife was a tall termagant, fierce of temper, loud of tongue, and strong of arm. Her voice was often heard in wordy warfare with her husband; and his face sometimes showed signs that their conflicts were not confined to words. No one ventured, however, to interfere between them. The lonely wayfarer shrunk within himself at the horrid clamour and clapper-clawing; eyed the den of discord askance; and hurried on his way, rejoicing, if a bachelor, in his celibacy.

One day that Tom Walker had been to a distant part of the neighbourhood, he took what he considered a short cut homeward, through the swamp. Like most short cuts, it was an ill-chosen route. The swamp was thickly grown with great gloomy pines and hemlocks, some of them ninety feet high, which made it dark at noonday, and a retreat for all the owls of the neighbourhood. It was full of pits and quagmires, partly covered with weeds and mosses, where the green surface often betrayed the traveller into a gulf of black, smothering mud: there were also dark and stagnant pools, the abodes of the tadpole, the bull-frog, and the water-snake; where the trunks of pines and hemlocks lay half drowned, half rotting, looking like alligators sleeping in the mire.

Tom had long been picking his way cautiously through this

treacherous forest; stepping from tuft to tuft of rushes and roots, which afforded precarious footholds among deep sloughs; or pacing carefully, like a cat, along the prostrate trunks of trees; startled now and then by the sudden screaming of the bittern, or the quacking of a wild-duck, rising on the wing from some solitary pool. At length he arrived at a piece of firm ground, which ran out like a peninsula into the deep bosom of the swamp. It had been one of the strongholds of the Indians during their wars with the first colonists. Here they had thrown up a kind of fort, which they had looked upon as almost impregnable, and had used as a place of refuge for their squaws and children. Nothing remained of the old Indian fort but a few embankments, gradually sinking to the level of the surrounding earth, and already overgrown in part by oaks and other forest trees, the foliage of which formed a contrast to the dark pines and hemlocks of the swamp.

It was late in the dusk of evening when Tom Walker reached the old fort, and he paused there a while to rest himself. Any one but he would have felt unwilling to linger in this lonely, melancholy place, for the common people had a bad opinion of it, from the stories handed down from the time of the Indian wars; when it was asserted that the savages held incantations here, and made sacrifices to the evil spirits.

Tom Walker, however, was not a man to be troubled with any fears of the kind. He reposed himself for some time on the trunk of a fallen hemlock, listening to the boding cry of the tree-toad, and delving with his walking-staff into a mound of black mould at his feet. As he turned up the soil unconsciously, his staff struck against something hard. He raked it out of the vegetable mould, and lo! a cloven skull, with an Indian tomahawk buried deep in it, lay before him. The rust on the weapon showed the time that had elapsed since this death-blow had been given. It was a dreary memento of the fierce struggle that had taken place in this last foothold of the Indian warriors.

'Humph!' said Tom Walker, as he gave it a kick to shake the dirt from it.

'Let that skull alone!' said a gruff voice. Tom lifted up his eyes, and beheld a great black man seated directly opposite him, on the stump of a tree. He was exceedingly surprised, having neither heard nor seen any one approach, and he was still more perplexed on observing, as well as the gathering gloom would permit, that the stranger was neither negro nor Indian. It is true he was dressed in a rude half Indian garb, and had a red belt or sash swathed round his body; but his face was neither black nor copper-colour, but swarthy and dingy, and begrimed with soot, as if he had been accustomed to toil among fires and forges. He had a shock of coarse black hair, that stood out from his head in all directions, and bore an axe on his shoulder.

He scowled for a moment at Tom with a pair of great red eyes.

'What are you doing on my grounds?' said the black man, with a hoarse growling voice.

'Your grounds!' said Tom with a sneer, 'no more your grounds than mine; they belong to Deacon Peabody.'

'Deacon Peabody be damned,' said the stranger, 'as I flatter myself he will be, if he does not look more to his own sins and less to those of his neighbours. Look yonder, and see how Deacon Peabody is faring.'

Tom looked in the direction that the stranger pointed, and beheld one of the great trees, fair and flourishing without, but rotten at the core, and saw that it had been nearly hewn through, so that the first high wind was likely to blow it down. On the bark of the tree was scored the name of Deacon Peabody, an eminent man, who had waxed wealthy by driving shrewd bargains with the Indians. He now looked round, and found most of the tall trees marked with the name of some great man of the colony, and all more or less scored with an axe. The one on which he had been seated, and which had evidently just been hewn down, bore the name of Crowninshield; and he recollected a mighty rich man of that name, who made a vulgar display of wealth, which it was whispered he had acquired by buccaneering.

'He's just ready for burning!' said the black man, with a growl of triumph. 'You see I am likely to have a good stock of firewood for winter.'

'But what right have you,' said Tom, 'to cut down Deacon Peabody's timber?'

'The right of a prior claim,' said the other. 'This woodland belonged to me long before one of your white-faced race put foot upon the soil.'

'And pray, who are you, if I may be so bold?' said Tom.

'Oh, I go by various names. I am the wild huntsman in some countries; the black miner in others. In this neighbourhood I am known by the name of the black woodsman. I am he to whom the red men consecrated this spot, and in honour of whom they now and then roasted a white man, by way of sweet-smelling sacrifice. Since the red men have been exterminated by you white savages, I amuse myself by presiding at the persecutions of Quakers and Anabaptists; I am the great patron and prompter of slave-dealers, and the grand-master of the Salem witches.'

'The upshot of all which is that, if I mistake not,' said Tom sturdily, 'you are he commonly called Old Scratch.'

'The same, at your service!' replied the black man, with a half civil nod.

Such was the opening of this interview, according to the old story; though it has almost too familiar an air to be credited. One would think that to meet with such a singular personage, in this wild, lonely place, would have shaken any man's nerves; but Tom was a hard-minded fellow, not easily daunted, and he had lived so long with a termagant wife, that he did not even fear the devil.

It is said that after this commencement they had a long and earnest conversation together, as Tom returned homeward. The black man told him of great sums of money buried by Kidd the pirate, under the oak-trees on the high ridge, not far from the morass. All these were under his command, and protected by his power, so that none could find them but such as propitiated his favour. These he offered to place within Tom Walker's reach, having conceived an especial kindness for him; but they were to be had only on certain conditions. What these conditions were may easily be surmised, though Tom never disclosed them publicly. They must have been very hard, for he required time to think of them, and he was not a man to stick at trifles where money was in view. When they had reached the edge of the swamp, the stranger paused.—'What proof have I that all you have been telling me is true?' said Tom. 'There is my signature,' said the black man, pressing his finger on Tom's forehead. So saying, he turned off among the thickets of the swamp, and seemed, as Tom said, to go down, down, down, into the earth, until nothing but his head and shoulders could be seen, and so on, until he totally disappeared.

When Tom reached home, he found the black print of a finger, burnt, as it were, into his forehead, which nothing could obliterate.

The first news his wife had to tell him was the sudden death of Absalom Crowninshield, the rich buccaneer. It was announced in the paper with the usual flourish, that 'A great man had fallen in Israel'.

Tom recollected the tree which his black friend had just hewn down, and which was ready for burning. 'Let the freebooter roast,' said Tom; 'who cares!' He now felt convinced that all he had heard and seen was no illusion.

He was not prone to let his wife into his confidence; but as this was an uneasy secret, he willingly shared it with her. All her avarice was awakened at the mention of hidden gold, and she urged her husband to comply with the black man's terms, and secure what would make them wealthy for life. However Tom might have felt disposed to sell himself to the devil, he was determined not to do so to oblige his wife; so he flatly refused, out of the mere spirit of contradiction. Many and bitter were the quarrels they had on the subject, but the more she talked, the more resolute was Tom not to be damned to please her.

At length she determined to drive the bargain on her own account, and, if she succeeded, to keep all the gain to herself. Being of the same fearless temper as her husband, she set off for the old Indian fort towards the close of a summer's day. She was many hours absent. When she came back, she was reserved and sullen in her replies. She spoke something of a black man, whom she had met about twilight, hewing at the root of a tall tree. He was sulky, however, and would not come to terms: she was to go again with a propitiatory offering, but what it was she forbore to say.

The next evening she set off again for the swamp, with her apron heavily laden. Tom waited and waited for her, but in vain; midnight came, but she did not make her appearance: morning, noon, night returned, but still she did not come. Tom now grew uneasy for her safety, especially as he found she had carried off in her apron the silver teapot and spoons, and every portable article of value. Another night elapsed, another morning came; but no wife. In a word, she was never heard of more.

What was her real fate nobody knows, in consequence of so many pretending to know. It is one of those facts which have become confounded by a variety of historians. Some asserted that she lost her way among the tangled mazes of the swamp, and sank into some pit or slough; others, more uncharitable, hinted that she had eloped with the household booty, and made off to some other province; while others surmised that the tempter had decoyed her into a dismal quagmire, on the top of which her hat was found lying. In confirmation of this, it was said a great black man, with an axe on his shoulder, was seen late that very evening coming out of the swamp, carrying a bundle tied in a check apron, with an air of surly triumph.

The most current and probable story, however, observes that Tom Walker grew so anxious about the fate of his wife and his property, that he set out at length to seek them both at the Indian fort. During a long summer's afternoon he searched about the gloomy place, but no wife was to be seen. He called her name repeatedly, but she was nowhere to be heard. The bittern alone responded to his voice, as he flew screaming by; or the bull-frog croaked dolefully from a neighbouring pool. At length, it is said, just in the brown hour of twilight, when the owls began to hoot, and the bats to flit about, his attention was attracted by the clamour of carrion crows hovering about a cypress-tree. He looked up, and beheld a bundle tied in a check apron, and hanging in the branches of the tree, with a great vulture perched hard by, as if keeping watch upon it. He leaped with joy; for he recognized his wife's apron, and supposed it to contain the household valuables.

'Let us get hold of the property,' said he, consolingly to himself, 'and we will endeavour to do without the woman.'

As he scrambled up the tree, the vulture spread its wide wings, and sailed off screaming into the deep shadows of the forest. Tom seized the check apron, but, woeful sight! found nothing but a heart and liver tied up in it!

Such, according to the most authentic old story, was all that was to be found of Tom's wife. She had probably attempted to deal with the black man as she had been accustomed to deal with her husband; but though a female scold is generally considered a match for the devil, yet in this instance she appears to have had the worst of it. She must have died game, however; for it is said Tom noticed many prints of cloven feet deeply stamped about the tree, and found handfuls of hair, that looked as if they had been plucked from the coarse black shock of the woodman. Tom knew his wife's prowess by experience. He shrugged his shoulders, as he looked at the signs of a fierce clapper-clawing. 'Egad,' said he to himself, 'Old Scratch must have had a tough time of it!'

Tom consoled himself for the loss of his property, with the loss of his wife, for he was a man of fortitude. He even felt something like gratitude towards the black woodman, who, he considered, had done him a kindness. He sought, therefore, to cultivate a further acquaintance with him, but for some time without success; the old blacklegs played shy, for, whatever people may think, he is not always to be had for calling for: he knows how to play his cards when pretty sure of his game.

At length, it is said, when delay had whetted Tom's eagerness to the quick, and prepared him to agree to anything rather than not gain the promised treasure, he met the black man one evening in his usual woodman's dress, with his axe on his shoulder, sauntering along the swamp, and humming a tune. He affected to receive Tom's advances with great indifference, made brief replies, and went on humming his tune.

By degrees, however, Tom brought him to business, and they began to haggle about the terms on which the former was to have the pirate's treasure. There was one condition which need not be mentioned, being generally understood in all cases where the devil grants favours; but there were others about which, though of less importance, he was inflexibly obstinate. He insisted that the money found through his means should be employed in his service. He proposed, therefore, that Tom should employ it in the black traffic; that is to say, that he should fit out a slave-ship. This however, Tom resolutely refused: he was bad enough in all conscience; but the devil himself could not tempt him to turn slave-trader.

Finding Tom so squeamish on this point, he did not insist upon it, but proposed, instead, that he should turn usurer; the devil being extremely anxious for the increase of usurers, looking upon them as his peculiar people.

To this no objections were made, for it was just to Tom's taste.

'You shall open a broker's shop in Boston next month,' said the black man.

'I'll do it tomorrow, if you wish,' said Tom Walker.

'You shall lend money at two per cent. a month.'

'Egad, I'll charge four!' replied Tom Walker.

'You shall extort bonds, foreclose mortgages, drive the merchant to bankruptcy. . . .'

'I'll drive him to the devil,' cried Tom Walker.

'You are the usurer for my money!' said the blacklegs with delight. 'When will you want the rhino?'

'This very night.'

'Done!' said the devil.

'Done!' said Tom Walker. So they shook hands and struck a bargain.

A few days' time saw Tom Walker seated behind his desk in a counting-house in Boston.

His reputation for a ready-moneyed man, who would lend money out for a good consideration, soon spread abroad. Everybody remembers the time of Governor Belcher, when money was particularly scarce. It was a time of paper credit.

The country had been deluged with government bills; the famous Land Bank had been established; there had been a rage for speculating; the people had run mad with schemes for new settlements; for building cities in the wilderness; land-jobbers went about with maps of grants, and townships, and Eldorados, lying nobody knew where, but which everybody was ready to purchase. In a word, the great speculating fever which breaks out every now and then in the country, had raged to an alarming degree, and everybody was dreaming of making sudden fortunes from nothing. As usual the fever had subsided; the dream had gone off, and the imaginary fortunes with it; the patients were left in doleful plight, and the whole country resounded with the consequent cry of 'hard times'.

At this propitious time of public distress did Tom Walker set up as usurer in Boston. His door was soon thronged by customers. The needy and adventurous; the gambling specu-lator; the dreaming land-jobber; the thriftless tradesman; the merchant with cracked credit; in short, every one driven to raise money by desperate means and desperate sacrifices, hurried to Tom Walker.

Thus Tom was the universal friend of the needy, and acted like a 'friend in need'; that is to say, he always exacted good pay and good security. In proportion to the distress of the applicant was the hardness of his terms. He accumulated bonds and mortgages; gradually squeezed his customers closer and closer: and sent them at length, dry as a sponge, from his door.

In this way he made money hand over hand; became a rich and mighty man, and exalted his cocked hat upon 'Change. He built himself, as usual, a vast house, out of ostentation; but left the greater part of it unfinished and unfurnished, out of parsimony. He even set up a carriage in the fullness of his vainglory, though he nearly starved the horses which drew it; and, as the ungreased wheels groaned and screeched on the axle-trees, you would have thought you heard the souls of the poor debtors he was squeezing.

As Tom waxed old, however, he grew thoughtful. Having secured the good things of this world, he began to feel anxious about those of the next. He thought with regret on the bargain he had made with his black friend, and set his wits to work to cheat him out of the conditions. He became, therefore, all of a sudden, a violent church-goer. He prayed loudly and strenuously, as if heaven were to be taken by force of lungs. Indeed, one might always tell when he had sinned most during the week, by the clamour of his Sunday devotion. The quiet Christians who had been modestly and steadfastly travelling Zion-ward, were struck with self-reproach at seeing themselves so suddenly outstripped in their career by this new-made convert. Tom was as rigid in religious as in money matters; he was a stern supervisor and censurer of his neighbours, and seemed to think every sin entered up to their account became a credit on his own side of the page. He even talked of the expediency of reviving the persecution of Quakers and Anabaptists. In a word, Tom's zeal became as notorious as his riches.

Still, in spite of all this strenuous attention to forms, Tom had a lurking dread that the devil, after all, would have his due. That he might not be taken unawares, therefore, it is said he always carried a small Bible in his coat-pocket. He had also a great folio Bible on his counting-house desk, and would frequently be found reading it when people called on business; on such occasions he would lay his green spectacles in the book, to mark the place, while he turned round to drive some usurious bargain.

Some say that Tom grew a little crack-brained in his old days, and that, fancying his end approaching, he had his horse new shod, saddled and bridled, and buried with his feet uppermost; because he supposed that at the last day the world would be turned upside down; in which case he should find his horse standing ready for mounting, and he was determined at the worst to give his old friend a run for it. This, however, is probably a mere old wives' fable. If he really did take such a precaution, it was totally superfluous; at least so says the authentic old legend, which closes his story in the following manner.

One hot summer afternoon in the dog-days, just as a terrible black thundergust was coming up, Tom sat in his counting-house in his white linen cap and India silk morning-gown. He was on the point of foreclosing a mortgage, by which he would complete the ruin of an unlucky land speculator for whom he had professed the greatest friendship. The poor land-jobber begged him to grant a few months' indulgence. Tom had grown testy and irritated, and refused another day.

'My family will be ruined and brought upon the parish,' said the land-jobber. 'Charity begins at home,' replied Tom; 'I must take care of myself in these hard times.'

'You have made so much money out of me,' said the speculator.

Tom lost his patience and his piety—'The devil take me,' said he, 'if I have made a farthing!'

Just then there were three loud knocks at the street door. He stepped out to see who was there. A black man was holding a black horse, which neighed and stamped with impatience.

'Tom, you're come for,' said the black fellow, gruffly. Tom shrunk back, but too late. He had left his little Bible at the bottom of his coat-pocket, and his big Bible on the desk buried under the mortgage he was about to foreclose: never was sinner taken more unawares. The black man whisked him like a child into the saddle, gave the horse a lash, and away he galloped, with Tom on his back, in the midst of the thunderstorm. The clerks stuck their pens behind their ears, and stared after him from the windows. Away went Tom Walker, dashing down the streets; his white cap bobbing up and down; his morning-gown fluttering in the wind, and his steed striking fire out of the pavement at every bound. When the clerks turned to look for the black man he had disappeared.

Tom Walker never returned to foreclose the mortgage. A countryman who lived on the border of the swamp, reported that in the height of the thundergust he had heard a great clattering of hoofs and a howling along the road, and running to the window caught sight of a figure, such as I have described, on a horse that galloped like mad across the fields, over the hills and down into the black hemlock swamp towards the old Indian fort; and that shortly after a thunderbolt falling in that direction seemed to set the whole forest in a blaze.

The good people of Boston shook their heads and shrugged their shoulders, but had been so much accustomed to witches and goblins and tricks of the devil, in all kinds of shapes from the first settlement of the colony, that they were not so much horror-struck as might have been expected. Trustees were appointed to take charge of Tom's effects. There was nothing, however, to administer upon. On searching his coffers all his bonds and mortgages were found reduced to cinders. In place of gold and silver his iron chest was filled with chips and shavings; two skeletons lay in his stable instead of his half-starved horses, and the very next day his great house took fire and was burnt to the ground.

Such was the end of Tom Walker and his ill-gotten wealth. Let all griping money-brokers lay this story to heart. The truth of it is not to be doubted. The very hole under the oak-trees, whence he dug Kidd's money, is to be seen to this day; and the neighbouring swamp and old Indian fort are often haunted in stormy nights by a figure on horseback, in morning-gown and white cap, which is doubtless the troubled spirit of the usurer. In fact, the story has resolved itself into a proverb, and is the origin of that popular saying, so prevalent throughout New England, of 'The Devil and Tom Walker'.

from *Tales of a Traveller*

LEGEND OF THE ENGULPHED CONVENT

At the dark and melancholy period when Don Roderick the Goth and his chivalry were overthrown on the banks of the Gaudalete, and all Spain was overrun by the Moors, great was the devastation of churches and convents throughout that pious kingdom. The miraculous fate of one of those holy piles is thus recorded in an authentic legend of those days.

On the summit of a hill, not very distant from the capital city of Toledo, stood an ancient convent and chapel, dedicated to the invocation of Saint Benedict, and inhabited by a sisterhood of Benedictine nuns. This holy asylum was confined to females of noble lineage. The younger sisters of the highest families were here given in religious marriage to their Saviour, in order that the portions of their elder sisters might be increased, and they enabled to make suitable matches on earth; or that the family wealth might go undivided to elder brothers, and the dignity of their ancient houses be protected from decay. The convent was renowned, therefore, for enshrining within its walls a sisterhood of the purest blood, the most immaculate virtue, and most resplendent beauty, of all Gothic Spain.

When the Moors overran the kingdom, there was nothing that more excited their hostility, than these virgin asylums. The very sight of a convent-spire was sufficient to set their Moslem blood in a ferment, and they sacked it with as fierce a zeal as though the sacking of a nunnery were a sure passport to Elysium.

Tidings of such outrages, committed in various parts of the kingdom, reached this noble sanctuary, and filled it with dismay. The danger came nearer and nearer; the infidel hosts were spreading all over the country; Toledo itself was captured; there was no flying from the convent, and no security within its walls.

In the midst of this agitation, the alarm was given one day, that a great band of Saracens were spurring across the plain. In an instant the whole convent was a scene of confusion. Some of the nuns wrung their fair hands at the windows; others waved their veils, and uttered shrieks from the tops of the towers, vainly hoping to draw relief from a country overrun by the foe. The sight of these innocent doves thus fluttering about their dovecote, but increased the zealot fury of the whiskered Moors. They thundered at the portal, and at every blow the ponderous gates trembled on their hinges.

The nuns now crowded round the abbess. They had been accustomed to look up to her as all-powerful, and they now implored her protection. The mother abbess looked with a rueful eye upon the treasures of beauty and vestal virtue exposed to such imminent peril. Alas! how was she to protect them from the spoiler! She had, it is true, experienced many signal interpositions of Providence in her individual favour. Her early days had been passed amid the temptations of a court, where her virtue had been purified by repeated trials, from none of which had she escaped but by miracle. But were miracles never to cease? Could she hope that the marvellous protection shown to herself would be extended to a whole sisterhood? There was no other resource. The Moors were at the threshold; a few moments more and the convent would be at their mercy. Summoning her nuns to follow her, she hurried into the chapel, and throwing herself on her knees before the image of the blessed Mary, 'Oh! holy Lady!' exclaimed she, 'oh, most pure and immaculate of virgins! thou seest our extremity. The ravager is at the gate, and there is none on earth to help us! Look down with pity, and grant that the earth may gape and swallow us, rather than that our cloister vows should suffer violation!'

The Moors redoubled their assault upon the portal; the gates gave way with a tremendous crash; a savage yell of exultation arose; when of a sudden the earth yawned; down sank the convent, with its cloisters, its dormitories and all its nuns. The chapel-tower was the last that sank, the bell ringing forth a peal of triumph in the very teeth of the infidels.

⟨❦⟩

Forty years had passed and gone, since the period of this miracle. The subjugation of Spain was complete. The Moors lorded it over city and country; and such of the Christian population as remained, and were permitted to exercise their religion, did it in humble resignation to the Moslem sway.

At this time a Christian cavalier of Cordova, hearing that a patriotic band of his countrymen had raised the standard of the Cross in the mountains of the Asturias, resolved to join them, and unite in breaking the yoke of bondage. Secretly arming himself, and caparisoning his steed, he set forth from Cordova, and pursued his course by unfrequented mule paths, and along the dry channels made by winter torrents. His spirit burned with indignation whenever, on commanding a view over a long sweeping plain, he beheld the mosque swelling in the distance, and the Arab horsemen careering about, as if the rightful lords of the soil. Many a deep-drawn sigh and heavy groan also, did the good cavalier utter, on passing the ruins of churches and convents desolated by the conquerors.

It was on a sultry midsummer evening that this wandering cavalier, in skirting a hill thickly covered with forest, heard the faint tones of a vesper bell, sounding melodiously in the air, and seeming to come from the summit of the hill. The cavalier crossed himself with wonder at this unwonted and Christian sound. He supposed it to proceed from one of those humble chapels and hermitages permitted to exist through the indulgence of the Moslem conquerors. Turning his steed up a narrow path of the forest, he sought this sanctuary, in hopes of finding a hospitable shelter for the night. As he advanced, the trees threw a deep gloom around him, and the bat flitted across his path. The bell ceased to toll, and all was silence.

Presently a choir of female voices came stealing sweetly through the forest, chanting the evening service to the solemn accompaniment of an organ. The heart of the good cavalier melted at the sound, for it recalled the happier days of his country. Urging forward his weary steed, he at length arrived at a broad grassy area, on the summit of the hill, surrounded by the forest. Here the melodious voices rose in full chorus, like the swelling of the breeze; but whence they came he could not tell. Sometimes they were before, sometimes behind him; sometimes in the air; sometimes as if from within the bosom of the earth. At length they died away, and a holy stillness settled on the place.

The cavalier gazed around with bewildered eye. There was neither chapel nor convent, nor humble hermitage, to be seen; nothing but a moss-grown stone pinnacle, rising out of the centre of the area, surmounted by a cross. The green sward appeared to have been sacred from the tread of man or beast, and the surrounding trees bent toward the cross, as if in adoration.

The cavalier felt a sensation of holy awe. He alighted, and tethered his steed on the skirts of the forest, where he might crop the tender herbage; then approaching the cross, he knelt and poured forth his evening prayers before this relic of the Christian days of Spain. His orisons being concluded, he laid himself down at the foot of the pinnacle, and reclining his head against one of the stones, fell into a deep sleep.

About midnight he was awakened by the tolling of a bell, and found himself lying before the gate of an ancient convent. A train of nuns passed by, each bearing a taper. He rose and followed them into the chapel; in the centre was a bier, on which lay the corpse of an aged nun. The organ performed a solemn requiem: the nuns joining in chorus. When the funeral service was finished, a melodious voice chanted. *'Requiescat in pace!'* — 'May she rest in peace!' The lights immediately vanished; the whole passed away as a dream, and the cavalier found himself at the foot of the cross, and beheld, by the faint rays of the rising moon, his steed quietly grazing near him.

When the day dawned he descended the hill, and following the course of a small brook, came to a cave, at the entrance of which was seated an ancient man in hermit's garb, with rosary and cross, and a beard that descended to his girdle. He was one of those holy anchorites permitted by the Moors to live unmolested in the dens and caves, and humble hermitages, and even to practise the rites of their religion. The cavalier, dismounting, knelt and craved a benediction. He then related all that had befallen him in the night, and besought the hermit to explain the mystery.

'What thou hast heard and seen, my son,' replied the other, 'is but a type and shadow of the woes of Spain.'

He then related the foregoing story of the miraculous deliverance of the convent.

'Forty years,' added the old man, 'have elapsed since this event, yet the bells of that sacred edifice are still heard, from time to time, sounding from underground, together with the pealing of the organ and the chanting of the choir. The Moors avoid this neighbourhood, as haunted ground, and the whole place, as thou mayest perceive, has become covered with a thick and lonely forest.'

The cavalier listened with wonder to the story. For three days and nights did he keep vigils with the holy man beside the cross, but nothing more was to be seen of nun or convent. It is supposed that, forty years having elapsed, the natural lives of all the nuns were finished, and the cavalier had beheld the obsequies of the last. Certain it is that from that time bell, and organ, and choral chant, have never more been heard.

The mouldering pinnacle, surmounted by the cross, remains an object of pious pilgrimage. Some say that it anciently stood in front of the convent, but others that it was the spire which remained above ground, when the main body of the building sank, like the topmast of some tall ship that has foundered. These pious believers maintain that the convent is miraculously preserved entire in the centre of the mountain, where, if proper excavations were made, it would be found, with all its treasures, and monuments, and shrines, and relics, and the tombs of its virgin nuns.

Should any one doubt the truth of this marvellous inter-position of the Virgin, to protect the vestal purity of her votaries, let him read the excellent work entitled 'España Triumphante', written by Fray Antonio de Santa Maria, a barefoot friar of the Carmelite order, and he will doubt no longer.

from *Wolfert's Roost*

THE LEGEND OF THE ENCHANTED SOLDIER

Every body has heard of the Cave of St. Cyprian at Salamanca, where in old times judicial astronomy, necromancy, chiromancy, and other dark and damnable arts were secretly taught by an ancient sacristan; or, as some will have it, by the devil himself, in that disguise. The cave has long been shut up and the very site of it forgotten; though, according to tradition, the entrance was somewhere about where the stone cross stands in the small square of the seminary of Carvajal; and this tradition appears in some degree corroborated by the circumstances of the following story.

There was at one time a student of Salamanca, Don Vincente by name, of that merry but mendicant class, who set out on the road to learning without a penny in pouch for the journey, and who, during college vacations, beg from town to town and village to village to raise funds to enable them to pursue their studies through the ensuing term. He was now about to set forth on his wanderings; and being somewhat musical, slung on his back a guitar with which to amuse the villagers, and pay for a meal or a night's lodgings.

As he passed by the stone cross in the seminary square, he pulled off his hat and made a short invocation to St. Cyprian, for good luck; when casting his eyes upon the earth, he perceived something glitter at the foot of the cross. On picking it up, it proved to be a seal ring of mixed metal, in which gold and silver appeared to be blended. The seal bore as a device two triangles crossing each other, so as to form a star. This device is said to be a cabbalistic sign, invented by King Solomon the wise, and of mighty power in all cases of enchantment; but the honest student, being neither sage nor conjurer, knew nothing of the matter. He took the ring as a present from St. Cyprian in reward of his prayer; slipped it on his finger, made a bow to the cross, and strumming his guitar, set off merrily on his wanderings.

The life of a mendicant student in Spain is not the most miserable in the world; especially if he has any talent at making himself agreeable. He rambles at large from village to village, and city to city, wherever curiosity or caprice may conduct him. The country curates, who, for the most part, have been mendicant students in their time, give him shelter for the night, and a comfortable meal, and often enrich him with several quartos, or half-pence in the morning. As he presents himself from door to door in the streets of the cities, he meets with no harsh rebuff, no chilling contempt, for there is no disgrace attending his mendicity, many of the most learned men in Spain having commenced their career in this manner; but if, like the student in question, he is a good looking varlet and a merry companion; and, above all, if he can play the guitar, he is sure of a hearty welcome among the peasants, and smiles and favours from their wives and daughters.

In this way, then, did our ragged and musical son of learning make his way over half the kingdom; with the fixed determination to visit the famous city of Granada before his return. Sometimes he was gathered for the night into the fold of some village pastor; sometimes he was sheltered under the humble but hospitable roof of the peasant. Seated at the cottage door with his guitar, he delighted the simple folk with his ditties; or striking up a fandango or bolero, set the brown country lads and lasses dancing in the mellow twilight. In the morning he departed with kind words from host and hostess, and kind looks and, peradventure, a squeeze of the hand from the daughter.

At length he arrived at the great object of his musical vagabondizing, the far-famed city of Granada, and hailed with wonder and delight its Moorish towers, its lovely vega and its snowy mountains glistering through a summer atmosphere. It is needless to say with what eager curiosity he entered its gates and wandered through its streets, and gazed upon its oriental monuments. Every female face peering through a window or beaming from a balcony was to him a Zorayda or a Zelinda, nor could he meet a stately dame on the Alameda but he was ready to fancy her a Moorish princess, and to spread his student's robe beneath her feet.

His musical talent, his happy humour, his youth and his good looks, won him a universal welcome in spite of his ragged robes, and for several days he led a gay life in the old Moorish capital and its environs. One of his occasional haunts was the fountain of Avellanos, in the valley of the Darro. It is one of the popular resorts of Granada, and has been so since the days of the Moors; and here the student had an opportunity of pursuing his studies of female beauty; a branch of study to which he was a little prone.

Here he would take his seat with his guitar, improvise love-ditties to admiring groups of *maños* and *majas*, or prompt with his music the ever ready dancers. He was thus engaged one evening, when he beheld a padre of the church advancing at whose approach every one touched the hat. He was evidently a man of consequence; he certainly was a mirror of good if not of holy living; robust and rosy-faced, and breathing at every pore, with the warmth of the weather and the exercise of the walk. As he passed along he would every now and then draw a maravedi out of his pocket and bestow it on a beggar, with an air of signal beneficence. 'Ah, the blessed father!' would be the cry; 'long life to him, and may he soon be a bishop!'

To aid his steps in ascending the hill he leaned gently now and then on the arm of a handmaid, evidently the pet-lamb of this kindest of pastors. Ah, such a damsel! Andalus from head to foot: from the rose in her hair, to the fairy shoe and lacework stocking; Andalus in every movement; in every undulation of the body:—ripe, melting Andalus!—But then so modest!—so shy!, with downcast eyes, listening to the words of the padre; or, if by chance she let flash a side glance, it was suddenly checked and her eyes once more cast to the ground.

The good padre looked benignantly on the company about the fountain, and took his seat with some emphasis on a stone bench, while the handmaid hastened to bring him a glass of sparkling water. He sipped it deliberately and with a relish, tempering it with one of those spongy pieces of frosted eggs and sugar so dear to Spanish epicures, and on returning the glass to the hand of the damsel pinched her cheek with infinite loving-kindness.

'Ah, the good pastor!' whispered the student to himself; 'what a happiness would it be to be gathered into his fold with such a pet-lamb for a companion!'

But no such good fare was likely to befall him. In vain he essayed those powers of pleasing which he had found so irresistible with country curates and country lasses. Never had he touched his guitar with such skill; never had he poured forth more soul-moving ditties, but he had no longer a country curate or country lass to deal with. The worthy priest evidently did not relish music, and the modest damsel never raised her eyes from the ground. They remained but a short time at the fountain; the good padre hastened their return to Granada. The damsel gave the student one shy glance in retiring; but it plucked the heart out of his bosom!

He inquired about them after they had gone. Padre Tomás was one of the saints of Granada, a model of regularity; punctual in his hour of rising; his hour of taking a paseo for an appetite; his hours of eating; his hour of taking his siesta; his hour of playing his game of tresillo, of an evening, with some of the dames of the Cathedral circle; his hour of supping, and his hour of retiring to rest, to gather fresh strength for another day's round of similar duties. He had an easy sleek mule for his riding; a matronly housekeeper skilled in preparing tit-bits for his table; and the pet lamb, to smooth his pillow at night and bring him his chocolate in the morning.

Adieu now to the gay. thoughtless life of the student; the side glance of a bright eye had been the undoing of him. Day and night he could not get the image of this modest damsel out of his mind. He sought the mansion of the padre. Alas! it was above the class of houses accessible to a strolling student like himself. The worthy padre had no sympathy with him; he had never been *Estudiante sopista*, obliged to sing for his supper. He blockaded the house by day, catching a glance of the damsel now and then as she appeared at a casement; but these glances only fed his flame without encouraging his hope. He serenaded her balcony at night, and at one time was flattered by the appearance of something white at a window. Alas, it was only the nightcap of the padre.

Never was lover more devoted; never damsel more shy: the poor student was reduced to despair. At length arrived the eve of St. John, when the lower classes of Granada swarm into the country, dance away the afternoon, and pass midsummer's night on the banks of the Darro and the Xenil. Happy are they who on this eventful night can wash their faces in those waters just as the Cathedral bell tells midnight; for at that precise moment they have a beautifying power. The student, having nothing to do, suffered himself to be carried away by the holiday-seeking throng until he found himself in the narrow valley of the Darro, below the lofty hill and ruddy towers of the Alhambra. The dry bed of the river; the rocks which border it; the terraced gardens which overhang it were alive with variegated groups, dancing under the vines and fig-trees to the sound of the guitar and castanets.

The student remained for some time in doleful dumps, leaning against one of the huge misshapen stone pomegranates which adorn the ends of the little bridge over the Darro. He cast a wistful glance upon the merry scene, where every cavalier had his dame; or, to speak more appropriately, every Jack his Jill; sighed at his own solitary state, a victim to the black eye of the most unapproachable of damsels, and repined at his ragged garb, which seemed to shut the gate of hope against him.

By degrees his attention was attracted to a neighbour equally solitary with himself. This was a tall soldier, of a stern aspect and grizzled beard, who seemed posted as a sentry at the opposite pomegranate. His face was bronzed by time; he was arrayed in ancient Spanish armour, with buckler and lance, and stood immovable as a statue. What surprised the student was, that though thus strangely equipped, he was totally unnoticed by the passing throng, albeit that many almost brushed against him.

'This is a city of old-time peculiarities,' thought the student, 'and doubtless this is one of them with which the inhabitants are too familiar to be surprised.' His own curiosity, however, was awakened, and being of a social disposition, he accosted the soldier.

'A rare old suit of armour that which you wear, comrade. May I ask what corps you belong to?'

The soldier gasped out a reply from a pair of jaws which seemed to have rusted on their hinges.

'The royal guard of Ferdinand and Isabella.'

'Santa Maria! Why, it is three centuries since that corps was in service.'

'And for three centuries have I been mounting guard. Now I trust my tour of duty draws to a close. Dost thou desire fortune?'

The student held up his tattered cloak in reply.

'I understand thee. If thou hast faith and courage, follow me, and thy fortune is made.'

'Softly, comrade, to follow thee would require small courage in one who has nothing to lose but life and an old guitar, neither of much value; but my faith is of a different matter, and not to be put in temptation. If it be any criminal act by which I am to mend my fortune, think not my ragged cloak will make me undertake it.'

The soldier turned on him a look of high displeasure. 'My sword,' said he, 'has never been drawn but in the cause of the faith and the throne. I am a *Cristiano viejo*, trust in me and fear no evil.'

The student followed him wondering. He observed that no one heeded their conversation, and that the soldier made his way through the various groups of idlers unnoticed, as if invisible.

Crossing the bridge, the soldier led the way by a narrow and steep path past a Moorish mill and aqueduct, and up the ravine which separates the domains of the Generalife from those of the Alhambra. The last ray of the sun shone upon the red battlements of the latter, which beetled far above; and the convent bells were proclaiming the festival of the ensuing day. The ravine was overshadowed by fig-trees, vines, and myrtles, and the outer towers and walls of the fortress. It was dark and lonely, and the twilight-loving bats began to flit about. At length the soldier halted at a remote and ruined tower, apparently intended to guard a Moorish aqueduct. He struck the foundation with the butt-end of his spear. A rumbling sound was heard, and the solid stones yawned apart, leaving an opening as wide as a door.

'Enter in the name of the Holy Trinity,' said the soldier, 'and fear nothing.' The student's heart quaked, but he made the sign of the cross, muttered his Ave Maria, and followed his mysterious guide into a deep vault cut out of the solid rock under the tower, and covered with Arabic inscriptions. The soldier pointed to a stone seat hewn along one side of the vault. 'Behold,' said he, 'my couch for three hundred years.' The bewildered student tried to force a joke. 'By the blessed St. Anthony,' said he, 'but you must have slept soundly, considering the hardness of your couch.'

'On the contrary, sleep has been a stranger to those eyes, incessant watchfulness has been my doom. Listen to my lot. I was one of the royal guards of Ferdinand and Isabella; but was taken prisoner by the Moors in one of their sorties, and confined a captive in this tower. When preparations were made to surrender the fortress to the Christian sovereigns, I was prevailed upon by an Alfaqui, a Moorish priest, to aid him in secreting some of the treasures of Boabdil in this vault. I was justly punished for my fault. The Alfaqui was an African necromancer, and by his infernal arts cast a spell upon me—to guard his treasures. Something must have happened to him, for he never returned, and here have I remained ever since, buried alive. Years and years have rolled away; earthquakes have shaken this hill; I have heard stone by stone of the tower above tumbling to the ground, in the natural operation of time; but the spell-bound walls of this vault set both time and earthquakes at defiance.

'Once every hundred years, on the festival of St. John, the enchantment ceases to have thorough sway; I am permitted to go forth and post myself upon the bridge of the Darro, where you met me, waiting until some one shall arrive who may have power to break this magic spell. I have hitherto mounted guard there in vain. I walk as in a cloud, concealed from mortal sight. You are the first to accost me for now three hundred years. I behold the reason. I see on your finger the seal-ring of Solomon the wise, which is proof against all enchantment. With you it remains to deliver me from this awful dungeon, or to leave me to keep guard here for another hundred years.'

The student listened to this tale in mute wonderment. He had heard many tales of treasure shut up under strong enchantment in the vaults of the Alhambra, but had treated them as fables. He now felt the value of the seal-ring, which had, in a manner, been given to him by St. Cyprian. Still, though armed by so potent a talisman, it was an awful thing to find himself tête-à-tête in such a place with an enchanted soldier, who, according to the laws of nature, ought to have been quietly in his grave for nearly three centuries.

A personage of this kind, however, was quite out of the ordinary run, and not to be trifled with, and he assured him he might rely upon his friendship and goodwill to do everything in his power for his deliverance.

'I trust to a motive more powerful than friendship,' said the soldier.

He pointed to a ponderous iron coffer, secured by locks inscribed with Arabic characters. 'That coffer,' said he, 'contains countless treasure in gold and jewels, and precious stones. Break the magic spell by which I am enthralled, and one half of this treasure shall be thine.'

'But how am I to do it?'

'The aid of a Christian priest, and a Christian maid is necessary. The priest to exorcise the powers of darkness; the damsel to touch this chest with the seal of Solomon. This must be done at night. But have a care. This is solemn work, and not to be effected by the carnal-minded. The priest must be a *Cristiano viejo*, a model of sanctity; and must mortify the flesh before he comes here, by a rigorous fast of four-and-twenty hours: and as to the maiden, she must be above reproach, and proof against temptation. Linger not in finding such aid. In three days my furlough is at an end; if not delivered before midnight of the third, I shall have to mount guard for another century.'

'Fear not,' said the student, 'I have in my eye the very priest and damsel you describe; but how am I to regain admission to this tower?'

'The seal of Solomon will open the way for thee.'

The student issued forth from the tower much more gaily than he had entered. The wall closed behind him, and remained solid as before.

The next morning he repaired boldly to the mansion of the priest, no longer a poor strolling student, thrumming his way with a guitar; but an ambassador from the shadowy world, with enchanted treasures to bestow. No particulars are told of his negotiation, excepting that the zeal of the worthy priest was easily kindled at the idea of rescuing an old soldier of the faith and a strong-box of King Chico from the very clutches of Satan; and then what alms might be dispensed, what churches built, and how many poor relatives enriched with the Moorish treasure!

As to the immaculate handmaid, she was ready to lend her hand, which was all that was required, to the pious work; and if a shy glance now and then might be believed, the ambassador began to find favour in her modest eyes.

The greatest difficulty, however, was the fast to which the good Padre had to subject himself. Twice he attempted it, and twice the flesh was too strong for the spirit. It was only on the third day that he was enabled to withstand the temptations of the cupboard; but it was still a question whether he would hold out until the spell was broken.

At a late hour of the night the party groped their way up the ravine by the light of a lantern, and bearing a basket with provisions for exorcising the demon of hunger so soon as the other demons should be laid in the Red Sea.

The seal of Solomon opened their way into the tower. They found the soldier seated on the enchanted strong-box, awaiting their arrival. The exorcism was performed in due style. The damsel advanced and touched the locks of the coffer with the seal of Solomon. The lid flew open; and such treasures of gold and jewels and precious stones as flashed upon the eye!

'Here's cut and come again!' cried the student, exultingly, as he proceeded to cram his pockets.

'Fairly and softly,' exclaimed the soldier. 'Let us get the coffer out entire, and then divide.'

They accordingly went to work with might and main; but it was a difficult task; the chest was enormously heavy, and had been imbedded there for centuries. While they were thus employed the good dominie drew on one side and made a vigorous onslaught on the basket, by way of exorcising the demon of hunger which was raging in his entrails. In a little while a fat capon was devoured, and washed down by a deep potation of Val de Peñas; and, by way of grace after meat, he gave a kind-hearted kiss to the pet lamb who waited on him. It was quietly done in a corner, but the tell-tale walls babbled it forth as if in triumph. Never was chaste salute more awful in its effects. At the sound the soldier gave a great cry of despair; the coffer, which was half raised, fell back in its place and was locked once more. Priest, student, and damsel, found themselves outside the tower, the wall of which closed with a thundering jar. Alas! the good Padre had broken his fast too soon!

When recovered from his surprise, the student would have re-entered the tower, but learnt to his dismay that the damsel, in her fright, had let fall the seal of Solomon; it remained within the vault.

In a word, the cathedral bell tolled midnight; the spell was renewed; the soldier was doomed to mount guard for another hundred years, and there he and the treasure remain to this day—and all because the kind-hearted Padre kissed his handmaid. 'Ah father! father!' said the student, shaking his head ruefully, as they returned down the ravine, 'I fear there was less of the saint than the sinner in that kiss!'

Thus ends the legend as far as it has been authenticated. There is a tradition, however, that the student had brought off treasure enough in his pocket to set him up in the world; that he prospered in his affairs, that the worthy Padre gave him the pet lamb in marriage, by way of amends for the blunder in the vault; that the immaculate damsel proved a pattern for wives as she had been for handmaids, and bore her husband a numerous progeny; that the first was a wonder; it was born seven months after her marriage, and though a seven months boy, was the sturdiest of the flock. The rest were all born in the ordinary course of time.

The story of the enchanted soldier remains one of the popular traditions of Granada, though told in a variety of ways; the common people affirm that he still mounts guard on mid-summer eve, beside the gigantic stone pomegranate on the Bridge of the Darro; but remains invisible excepting to such lucky mortal as may possess the seal of Solomon.

from *The Alhambra*

GOVERNOR MANCO AND THE SOLDIER

When Governor Manco, or 'the one-armed', kept up a show of military state in the Alhambra, he became nettled at the reproaches continually cast upon his fortress, of being a nestling place of rogues and contrabandistas. On a sudden, the old potentate determined on reform, and setting vigorously to work, ejected whole nests of vagabonds out of the fortress and the gipsy caves with which the surrounding hills are honeycombed. He sent out soldiers also, to patrol the avenues and footpaths, with orders to take up all suspicious persons.

One bright summer morning, a patrol, consisting of the testy old corporal who had distinguished himself in the affair of the notary, a trumpeter and two privates, was seated under the garden wall of the Generalife, beside the road which leads down from the mountain of the sun, when they heard the tramp of a horse, and a male voice singing in rough, though not unmusical tones, an old Castilian campaigning song.

Presently they beheld a sturdy sun-burnt fellow, clad in the ragged garb of a foot soldier leading a powerful Arabian horse, caparisoned in the ancient Moresco fashion.

Astonished at the sight of a strange soldier descending, steed in hand, from that solitary mountain, the corporal stepped forth and challenged him.

'Who goes there?'

'A friend.'

'Who and what are you?'

'A poor soldier just from the wars, with a cracked crown and empty purse for a reward.'

By this time they were enabled to view him more narrowly. He had a black patch across his forehead, which, with a grizzled beard, added to a certain dare-devil cast of countenance, while a slight squint threw into the whole an occasional gleam of roguish good-humour.

Having answered the questions of the patrol, the soldier seemed to consider himself entitled to make others in return. 'May I ask,' said he, 'what city is that which I see at the foot of the hill?'

'What city!' cried the trumpeter; 'come, that's too bad. Here's a fellow lurking about the mountain of the sun, and demands the name of the great city of Granada!'

'Granada! Madre di Dios! can it be possible?'

'Perhaps not!' rejoined the trumpeter; 'and perhaps you have no idea that yonder are the towers of the Alhambra.'

'Son of a trumpet,' replied the stranger, 'do not trifle with me; if this be indeed the Alhambra, I have some strange matters to reveal to the governor.'

'You will have an opportunity,' said the corporal, 'for we mean to take you before him.' By this time the trumpeter had seized the bridle of the steed, the two privates had each secured an arm of the soldier, the corporal put himself in front, gave the word, 'Forward—march!' and away they marched for the Alhambra.

The sight of a ragged foot soldier and a fine Arabian horse, brought in captive by the patrol, attracted the attention of all the idlers of the fortress, and of those gossip groups that generally assemble about wells and fountains at early dawn. The wheel of the cistern paused in its rotations, and the slipshod servant-maid stood gaping, with pitcher in hand, as the corporal passed by with his prize. A motley train gradually gathered in the rear of the escort.

Knowing nods and winks and conjectures passed from one to another. 'It is a deserter,' said one; 'A contrabandista,' said another; 'A bandalero,' said a third;—until it was affirmed that a captain of a desperate band of robbers had been captured by the prowess of the corporal and his patrol. 'Well, well,' said the old crones, one to another, 'captain or not, let him get out of the grasp of old Governor Manco if he can, though he is but one-handed.'

Governor Manco was seated in one of the inner halls of the Alhambra, taking his morning's cup of chocolate in company with his confessor, a fat Franciscan friar, from the neighbouring convent. A demure, dark-eyed damsel of Malaga, the daughter of his housekeeper, was attending upon him. The world hinted that the damsel, who, with all her demureness, was a sly buxom baggage, had found out a soft spot in the iron heart of the old governor, and held complete control over him. But let that pass—the domestic affairs of these mighty potentates of the earth should not be too narrowly scrutinized.

When word was brought that a suspicious stranger had been taken lurking about the fortress, and was actually in the outer court, in durance of the corporal, waiting the pleasure of his excellency, the pride and stateliness of office swelled the bosom of the governor. Giving back his chocolate cup into the hands of the demure damsel, he called for his basket-hilted sword, girded it to his side, twirled up his mustachios, took his seat in a large high-backed chair, assumed a bitter and forbidding aspect, and ordered the prisoner into his presence. The soldier was brought in, still closely pinioned by his captors, and guarded by the corporal. He maintained, however, a resolute self-confident air, and returned the sharp, scrutinizing look of the governor with an easy squint, which by no means pleased the punctilious old potentate.

'Well, culprit,' said the governor, after he had regarded him for a moment in silence, 'what have you to say for yourself—who are you?'

'A soldier, just from the wars, who has brought away nothing but scars and bruises.'

'A soldier—humph—a foot soldier by your garb. I understand you have a fine Arabian horse. I presume you brought him too from the wars, beside your scars and bruises.'

'May it please your excellency, I have something strange to tell about the horse. Indeed I have one of the most wonderful things to relate. Something too that concerns the security of this fortress, indeed of all Granada. But it is a matter to be imparted only to your private ear, or in presence of such only as are in your confidence.'

The governor considered for a moment, and then directed the corporal and his men to withdraw, but to post themselves outside the door, and be ready at a call. 'This holy friar,' said he, 'is my confessor, you may say anything in his presence—and this damsel,' nodding towards the handmaid, who had loitered with an air of great curiosity, 'this damsel is of great secrecy and discretion, and to be trusted with anything.'

The soldier gave a glance between a squint and a leer at the demure handmaid. 'I am perfectly willing,' said he, 'that the damsel should remain.'

When all the rest had withdrawn, the soldier commenced his story. He was a fluent, smooth-tongued varlet, and had a command of language above his apparent rank.

'May it please your excellency,' said he, 'I am, as I before observed, a soldier, and have seen some hard service, but my term of enlistment being expired, I was discharged, not long since, from the army of Valladolid, and set out on foot for my native village in Andalusia. Yesterday evening the sun went down as I was traversing a great dry plain of Old Castile.

'Hold,' cried the governor, 'what is this you say? Old Castile is some two or three hundred miles from this.'

'Even so,' replied the soldier coolly. 'I told your excellency I had strange things to relate; but not more strange than true; as your excellency will find, if you will deign me a patient hearing.'

'Proceed, culprit,' said the governor, twirling up his mustachios.

'As the sun went down,' continued the soldier, 'I cast my eyes about in search of some quarters for the night; but, far as my sight could reach, there were no signs of habitation. I saw that I should have to make my bed on the naked plain, with my knapsack for a pillow; but your excellency is an old soldier, and knows that to one who has been in the wars such a night's lodging is no great hardship.'

The governor nodded assent, as he drew his pocket handkerchief out of the basket hilt, to drive away a fly that buzzed about his nose.

'Well, to make a long story short,' continued the soldier, 'I trudged forward for several miles until I came to a bridge over a deep ravine, through which ran a little thread of water, almost dried up by the summer heat. At one end of the bridge was a Moorish tower, the upper end all in ruins, but a vault in the foundation quite entire. Here, thinks I, is a good place to make a halt; so I went down to the stream, took a hearty drink, for the water was pure and sweet, and I was parched with thirst; then opening my wallet, I took out an onion and a few crusts, which were all my provisions, and seating myself on a stone on the margin of the stream, began to make my supper; intending afterwards to quarter myself for the night in the vault of the tower; and capital quarters they would have been for a campaigner just from the wars, as your excellency, who is an old soldier, may suppose.'

'I have put up gladly with worse in my time,' said the governor, returning his pocket handkerchief into the hilt of his sword.

'While I was quietly crunching my crust,' pursued the soldier, 'I heard something stir within the vault; I listened—it was the tramp of a horse. By-and-by, a man came forth from a door in the foundation of the tower, close by the water's edge, leading a powerful horse by the bridle. I could not well make out what he was by the starlight. It had a suspicious look to be lurking among the ruins of a tower, in that wild solitary place. He might be a mere wayfarer, like myself; he might be a contrabandista; he might be a bandalero; what of that? thank heaven and my poverty, I had nothing to lose; so I sat still and crunched my crusts.

'He led his horse to the water, close by where I was sitting, so that I had a fair opportunity of reconnoitring him. To my surprise, he was dressed in a Moorish garb, with a cuirass of steel, and a polished skull-cap that I distinguished by the reflection of the stars upon it. His horse, too, was harnessed in the Moresco fashion, with great shovel stirrups. He led him, as I said, to the side of the stream, into which the animal plunged his head almost to the eyes, and drank until I thought he would have burst.

'"Comrade," said I, "your steed drinks well; it's a good sign when a horse plunges his muzzle bravely into the water."

'"He may well drink," said the stranger, speaking with a Moorish accent, "it is a good year since he had his last draught."

'"By Santiago," said I, "that beats even the camels that I have seen in Africa. But come, you seem to be something of a soldier, will you sit down and take part of a soldier's fare?" In fact I felt the want of a companion in this lonely place, and was willing to put up with an infidel. Besides, as your excellency well knows, a soldier is never very particular about the faith of his company, and soldiers of all countries are comrades on peaceable ground.'

The governor again nodded assent.

'Well, as I was saying, I invited him to share my supper, such as it was, for I could not do less in common hospitality. "I have no time to pause for meat or drink," said he, "I have a long journey to make before morning."

'"In which direction?" said I.

'"Andalusia," said he.

'"Exactly my route," said I; "so, as you won't stop and eat with me, perhaps you will let me mount and ride with you. I see your horse is of a powerful frame, I'll warrant he'll carry double."

'"Agreed," said the trooper; and it would not have been civil and soldier-like to refuse, especially as I had offered to share my supper with him. So up he mounted, and up I mounted behind him.

'"Hold fast," said he, "my steed goes like the wind."

'"Never fear me," said I, and so off we set.

'From a walk the horse soon passed to a trot, from a trot to a gallop, and from a gallop to a harum scarum scamper. It seemed as if rocks, trees, houses, everything, flew hurry scurry behind us.

'"What town is this?" said I.

'"Segovia," said he; and before the word was out of his mouth, the towers of Segovia were out of sight. We swept up the Guadarama mountains, and down by the Escurial; and we skirted the walls of Madrid, and we scoured away across the plains of La Mancha. In this way we went up hill and down dale, by towers and cities, all buried in deep sleep, and across mountains, and plains, and rivers, just glimmering in the starlight.

'To make a long story short, and not to fatigue your excellency, the trooper suddenly pulled up on the side of a mountain. "Here we are," said he, "at the end of our journey." I looked about, but could see no signs of habitation; nothing but the mouth of a cavern. While I looked I saw multitudes of people in Moorish dresses, some on horseback, some on foot, arriving as if borne by the wind from all points of the compass, and hurrying into the mouth of the cavern, like bees into a hive. Before I could ask a question, the trooper struck his long Moorish spurs into the horse's flanks and dashed in with the throng. We passed along a steep winding way, that descended into the very bowels of the mountain. As we pushed on, a light began to glimmer up by little and little, like the first glimmerings of day, but what caused it I could not discern. It grew stronger and stronger, and enabled me to see everything around. I now noticed, as we passed along, great caverns, opening to the right and left, like halls in an arsenal. In some there were shields, and helmets, and cuirasses, and lances, and scimitars, hanging against the walls; in others there were great heaps of warlike munitions, and camp equipage lying upon the ground.

'It would have done your excellency's heart good, being an old soldier, to have seen such grand provision for war. Then, in other caverns, there were long rows of horsemen armed to the teeth, with lances raised and banners unfurled all ready for the field; but they all sat motionless in their saddles like so many statues. In other halls were warriors sleeping on the ground beside their horses, and foot-soldiers in groups ready to fall into the ranks. All were in old-fashioned Moorish dresses and armour.

'Well, your excellency, to cut a long story short, we at length entered an immense cavern, or I may say palace, of grotto work, the walls of which seemed to be veined with gold and silver, and to sparkle with diamonds and sapphires and all kinds of precious stones. At the upper end sat a Moorish king on a golden throne, with his nobles on each side, and a guard of African blacks with drawn scimitars. All the crowd that continued to flock in, and amounted to thousands and thousands, passed one by one before his throne, each paying homage as he passed. Some of the multitude were dressed in magnificent robes, without stain or blemish, and sparkling with jewels; others in burnished and enamelled armour; while others were in mouldered and mildewed garments, and in armour all battered and dented and covered with rust.

'I had hitherto held my tongue, for your excellency well knows, it is not for a soldier to ask many questions when on duty, but I could keep silent no longer.

'"Pr'ythee, comrade," said I, "what is the meaning of all this?"

'"This," said the trooper, "is a great and fearful mystery. Know, O Christian, that you see before you the court and army of Boabdil the last king of Granada."

'"What is this you tell me?" I cried. "Boabdil and his court were exiled from the land hundreds of years agone, and all died in Africa."

'"So it is recorded in your lying chronicles," replied the Moor: "but know that Boabdil and the warriors who made the last struggle for Granada were all shut up in the mountain by powerful enchantment. As for the king and army that marched forth from Granada at the time of the surrender, they were a mere phantom train, of spirits and demons permitted to assume those shapes to deceive the Christian sovereigns. And further-more let me tell you, friend, that all Spain is a country under the power of enchantment. There is not a mountain cave, not a lonely watch-tower in the plains, nor ruined castle on the hills, but has some spellbound warriors sleeping from age to age within its vaults, until the sins are expiated for which Allah permitted the dominion to pass for a time out of the hands of the faithful. Once every year, on the eve of St. John, they are released from enchantment, from sunset to sunrise, and permitted to repair here to pay homage to their sovereign: and the crowds which you beheld swarming into the cave are Moslem warriors from their haunts in all parts of Spain. For my own part, you saw the ruined tower of the bridge in Old Castile, where I have now wintered and summered for many hundred years, and where I must be back again by daybreak. As to the battalions of horse and foot which you beheld draw up in array in the neighbouring caverns, they are the spell-bound warriors of Granada. It is written in the book of fate, that when the enchantment is broken, Boabdil will descend from the mountain at the head of this army, resume his throne in the Alhambra and his sway of Granada, and gathering together the enchanted warriors, from all parts of Spain, will reconquer the peninsula and restore it to Moslem rule."

'"And when shall this happen?" said I.

'"Allah alone knows: we had hoped the day of deliverance was at hand; but there reigns at present a vigilant governor in the Alhambra, a stanch old soldier, well known as Governor Manco. While such a warrior holds command of the very outpost, and stands ready to check the first irruption from the mountain, I fear Boabdil and his soldiery must be content to rest upon their arms."'

Here the governor raised himself somewhat perpendicularly, adjusted his sword, and twirled up his mustachios.

'To make a long story short, and not to fatigue your excellency, the trooper, having given me this account, dismounted from his steed.

'"Tarry here," said he, "and guard my steed while I go and bow the knee to Boabdil." So saying, he strode away among the throng that pressed forward to the throne.

'"What's to be done?" thought I, when thus left to myself; "shall I wait here until this infidel returns to whisk me off on his goblin steed, the Lord knows where; or shall I make the most of my time and beat a retreat from this hobgoblin community?" A soldier's mind is soon made up, as your excellency well knows. As to the horse, he belonged to an avowed enemy of the faith and the realm, and was a fair prize according to the rules of war. So hoisting myself from the crupper into the saddle, I turned the reins, struck the Moorish stirrups into the sides of the steed, and put him to make the best of his way out of the passage by which he had entered. As we scoured by the halls where the Moslem horsemen sat in motionless battalions, I thought I heard the clang of armour and a hollow murmur of voices. I gave the steed another taste of the stirrups and doubled my speed. There was now a sound behind me like a rushing blast; I heard the clatter of a thousand hoofs: a countless throng overtook me. I was borne along in the press, and hurled forth from the mouth of the cavern, while thousands of shadowy forms were swept off in every direction by the four winds of heaven.

'In the whirl and confusion of the scene I was thrown senseless to the earth. When I came to myself I was lying on the brow of a hill with the Arabian steed standing beside me; for, in falling, my arm had slipt within the bridle, which, I presume, prevented his whisking off to Old Castile.

'Your excellency may easily judge of my surprise on looking round, to behold hedges of aloes and Indian figs and other proofs of a southern climate, and to see a great city below me with towers, and palaces, and a grand cathedral.

'I descended the hill cautiously, leading my steed, for I was afraid to mount him again, lest he should play me some slippery trick. As I descended I met with your patrol, who let me into the secret that it was Granada that lay before me; and that I was actually under the walls of the Alhambra, the fortress of the redoubted Governor Manco, the terror of all enchanted Moslems. When I heard this, I determined at once to seek your excellency, to inform you of all that I had seen, and to warn you of the perils that surround and undermine you, that you may take measures in time to guard your fortress, and the kingdom itself, from this intestine army that lurks in the very bowels of the land.'

'And pr'ythee, friend, you who are a veteran campaigner, and have seen so much service,' said the governor, 'how would you advise me to proceed, in order to prevent this evil?'

'It is not for a humble private of the ranks,' said the soldier modestly, 'to pretend to instruct a commander of your excellency's sagacity, but it appears to me that your excellency might cause all the caves and entrances in the mountain to be walled up with solid mason work, so that Boabdil and his army might be completely corked up in their subterranean habitation. If the good father too,' added the soldier reverently bowing to the friar, and devoutly crossing himself, 'would consecrate the barricadoes with his blessing, and put up a few crosses and reliques and images of saints, I think they might withstand all the power of infidel enchantments.'

'They doubtless would be of great avail,' said the friar.

The governor now placed his arm akimbo with his hand resting on the hilt of his toledo, fixing his eye upon the soldier, and gently wagging his head from one side to the other.

'So, friend,' said he, 'then you really suppose I am to be gulled with this cock-and-bull story about enchanted mountains and enchanted Moors? Hark ye, culprit!—not another word. An old soldier you may be, but you'll find you have an older soldier to deal with, and one not easily outgeneralled. Ho! guards there! put this fellow in irons.'

The demure handmaid would have put in a word in favour of the prisoner, but the governor silenced her with a look.

As they were pinioning the soldier, one of the guards felt something of bulk in his pocket, and drawing it forth, found a long leathern purse that appeared to be well filled. Holding it by one corner, he turned out the contents upon the table before the governor, and never did freebooter's bag make more gorgeous delivery. Out tumbled rings, and jewels, and rosaries of pearls, and sparkling diamond crosses, and a profusion of ancient golden coin, some of which fell jingling to the floor, and rolled away to the uttermost parts of the chamber.

For a time the functions of justice were suspended; there was a universal scramble after the glittering fugitives. The governor alone, who was imbued with true Spanish pride, maintained his stately decorum, though his eye betrayed a little anxiety until the last coin and jewel were restored to the sack.

The friar was not so calm; his whole face glowed like a furnace, and his eyes twinkled and flashed at sight of the rosaries and crosses.

'Sacrilegious wretch that thou art!' exclaimed he; 'what church or sanctuary hast thou been plundering of these sacred relics?'

'Neither one nor the other, holy father. If they be sacrilegious spoils, they must have been taken in times long past, by the infidel trooper I have mentioned. I was just going to tell his excellency when he interrupted me, that, on taking possession of the trooper's horse, I unhooked a leathern sack which hung at the saddle-bow, and which I presume contained the plunder of his campaignings in days of old, when the Moors overran the country.'

'Mighty well; at present you will make up your mind to take up your quarters in a chamber of the vermilion tower, which, though not under a magic spell, will hold you as safe as any cave of your enchanted Moors.'

'Your excellency will do as you think proper,' said the prisoner coolly. 'I shall be thankful to your excellency for any accommodation in the fortress. A soldier who has been in the wars, as your excellency well knows, is not particular about his lodgings: provided I have a snug dungeon and regular rations, I shall manage to make myself comfortable. I would only entreat that while your excellency is so careful about me, you would have an eye to your fortress, and think on the hint I dropped about stopping up the entrances to the mountain.'

Here ended the scene. The prisoner was conducted to a strong dungeon in the vermilion tower, the Arabian steed was led to his excellency's stable, and the trooper's sack was deposited in his excellency's strong box. To the latter, it is true, the friar made some demur, questioning whether the sacred relics, which were evidently sacrilegious spoils, should not be placed in custody of the church; but as the governor was peremptory on the subject, and was absolute lord in the Alhambra, the friar discreetly dropped the discussion, but determined to convey intelligence of the fact to the church dignitaries in Granada.

To explain these prompt and rigid measures on the part of old Governor Manco, it is proper to observe, that about this time the Alpuxarra mountains in the neighbourhood of Granada were terribly infested by a gang of robbers, under the command of a daring chief, named Manuel Borasco, who were accustomed to prowl about the country, and even to enter the city in various disguises, to gain intelligence of the departure of convoys of merchandise, or travellers with well-lined purses, whom they took care to waylay in distant and solitary passes of their road. These repeated and daring outrages had awakened the attention of government, and the commanders of the various posts had received instructions to be on the alert, and to take up all suspicious stragglers. Governor Manco was particularly zealous in consequence of the various stigmas that had been cast upon his fortress, and he now doubted not that he had entrapped some formidable desperado of this gang.

In the meantime the story took wind, and became the talk, not merely of the fortress, but of the whole city of Granada. It was said that the noted robber Manuel Borasco, the terror of the Alpuxarras, had fallen into the clutches of old Governor Manco, and been cooped up by him in a dungeon of the vermilion tower; and everyone who had been robbed by him flocked to recognise the marauder. The vermilion tower, as is well known, stands apart from the Alhambra on a sister hill, separated from the main fortress by the ravine down which passes the main avenue. There were no outer walls, but a sentinel patrolled before the tower. The window of the chamber in which the soldier was confined was strongly grated, and looked upon a small esplanade. Here the good folks of Granada repaired to gaze at him, as they would at a laughing hyena, grinning through the cage of a menagerie. Nobody, however, recognised him for Manuel Borasco; for that terrible robber was noted for a ferocious physiognomy, and had by no means the good-humoured squint of the prisoner. Visitors came not merely from the city, but from all parts of the country; but nobody knew him, and there began to be doubts in the minds of the common people whether there might not be some truth in his story. That Boabdil and his army were shut up in the mountain, was an old tradition which many of the ancient inhabitants had heard from their fathers. Numbers went up to the mountain of the sun, or rather to St. Elena, in search of the cave mentioned by the soldier; and saw and peeped into the deep dark pit, descending, no one knows how far, into the mountain, and which remains there to this day—the fabled entrance to the subterranean abode of Boabdil.

By degrees the soldier became popular with the common people. A freebooter of the mountains is by no means the opprobrious character in Spain that a robber is in any other country; on the contrary, he is a kind of chivalrous personage in the eyes of the lower classes. There is always a disposition, also, to cavil at the conduct of those in command; and many began to murmur at the high-handed measures of old Governor Manco, and to look upon the prisoner in the light of a martyr.

The soldier, moreover, was a merry, waggish fellow, that had a joke for everyone who came near his window, and a soft speech for every female. He had procured an old guitar also, and would sit by his window and sing ballads and love ditties, to the delight of the women of the neighbourhood, who would assemble on the esplanade in the evenings and dance boleros to his music. Having trimmed off his rough beard, his sunburnt face found favour in the eyes of the fair; and the demure handmaid of the governor declared that his squint was perfectly irresistible. This kind-hearted damsel had, from the first, evinced a deep sympathy in his fortunes, and having in vain tried to mollify the governor, had set to work privately to mitigate the rigour of his dispensations. Every day she brought the prisoner some crumbs of comfort which had fallen from the governor's table, or been abstracted from his larder, together with, now and then, a consoling bottle of choice Val de Peñas, or rich Malaga.

While this petty treason was going on, in the very centre of the old governor's citadel, a storm of open war was brewing up among his external foes. The circumstance of a bag of gold and jewels having been found upon the person of the supposed robber had been reported, with many exaggerations, in Granada. A question of territorial jurisdiction was immediately started by the governor's inveterate rival, the captain general. He insisted that the prisoner had been captured without the precincts of the Alhambra, and within the rules of his authority. He demanded his body therefore, and the *spolia opima* taken with him. Due information having been carried likewise by the friar to the grand Inquisitor of the crosses and rosaries, and other reliques contained in the bag, he claimed the culprit as having been guilty of sacrilege, and insisted that his plunder was due to the church, and his body to the next auto da fe. The feuds ran high, the governor was furious, and swore, rather than surrender his captive, he would hang him up within the Alhambra, as a spy caught within the purlieus of the fortress.

The captain general threatened to send a body of soldiers to transfer the prisoner from the vermilion tower to the city. The grand Inquisitor was equally bent upon despatching a number of the familiars of the Holy Office. Word was brought late at night to the governor of these machinations. 'Let them come,' said he, 'they'll find me beforehand with them; he must rise bright and early who would take in an old soldier.' He accordingly issued orders to have the prisoner removed at daybreak, to the donjon keep within the walls of the Alhambra. 'And d'ye hear, child,' said he to his demure handmaid, 'tap at my door, and wake me before cock-crowing, that I may see to the matter myself.'

The day dawned, the cock crowed, but nobody tapped at the door of the governor. The sun rose high above the mountain tops, and glittered in at his casement, ere the governor was wakened from his morning dreams by his veteran corporal, who stood before him with terror stamped upon his iron visage.

'He's off! he's gone!' cried the corporal, gasping for breath.

'Who's off—who's gone?'

'The soldier—the robber—the devil, for aught I know; his dungeon is empty, but the door locked,—no one knows how he has escaped out of it.'

'Who saw him last?'

'Your handmaid, she brought him his supper.'

'Let her be called instantly.'

Here was new matter of confusion. The chamber of the demure damsel was likewise empty, her bed had not been slept in: she had doubtless gone off with the culprit, as she had appeared, for some days past, to have frequent conversations with him.

This was wounding the old governor in a tender part; but he had scarce time to wince at it, when new misfortunes broke upon his view. On going into his cabinet he found his strong box open, the leather purse of the trooper abstracted, and with it, a couple of corpulent bags of doubloons.

But how, and which way, had the fugitives escaped? An old peasant who lived in a cottage by the road-side, leading up into the Sierra, declared that he had heard the tramp of a powerful steed just before daybreak, passing up into the mountains. He had looked out at his casement, and could just distinguish a horseman, with a female seated before him.

'Search the stables!' cried Governor Manco. The stables were searched; all the horses were in their stalls, excepting the Arabian steed. In his place was a stout cudgel tied to the manger, and on it a label bearing these words, 'A gift to Governor Manco, from an Old Soldier.'

from *The Alhambra*